# WHISTLER'S BROTHER

NANCY ELVIRA

Copyright © 2017 Nancy Elvira
ISBN 978-0-692-31926-0

Cover Design by Julie D. Womack


Cover Photographs

*"Tugging Down the River"* © Nancy Womack

"Man on Black" ©
Jos Temprano – Thinkstock


*Manufactured in the United States of America*

*"Tomorrow is the first page of your new story.
Write a good one."*

# WHISTLER'S
# BROTHER

## ~ *One* ~

*August, 1895*

JOHN'S HOLD ON HIS little brother tightened.

*"Uncle! Okay, you win!"* "Okay, okay – I won't tell her! I swear I won't! *Just let go!*"

John slowly released William's arm from his grip; Will slid to the grass and looked up at him, rubbing his arm as if a spasm of pain had shot through his entire body.

"That should teach you – and, mind you Will, that's just a warning," John said as he assisted his younger sibling back to his feet. He brushed the dirt from the knees of William's knickers and he continued walking along the dirt road. Will ran to catch up with him.

"I thought you *liked* Jennie," he wheezed, out of breath.

John smiled, half-embarrassed at the innocent question. He understood that his nine-year-old brother truly couldn't relate to the goings on in the courtship ritual of a man of seventeen years. He stopped and turned to William.

"Will – of course I fancy her. But that does not mean I want *her* to know that!" Then he messed up Will's hair and he smiled. "Yet."

Little clouds of dust filled the air as they continued along the narrow and cracked dirt road. William looked up at John in adoration of his older brother, wondering how he could be so smart; and be right about everything.

After supper, John found Will at the pond, staring up at the heavens. It was an ordinary evening in August - nothing strange or dramatic in the sky except for a few lingering rain clouds that quickly dissipated. He smiled and observed his brother while leaning back against the tree Will had curiously named *Orion*.

His little brother loved astronomy. By the time he was four years old, he had established a simple nightly ritual of counting the stars in the sky. And within a few more years, he had advanced to pointing out the Milky Way on clear nights or a planet when he recognized it sparkling in the sky.

Will and John each had different ideas of what they wanted to do with their lives. John chuckled at the thought – Will wanted to visit the moon and stars, while John wanted to travel the earth.

All those years of getting lost in the quiet of Illinois farm life; he had been assured that this was truly paradise. Indeed, it may have been paradise … for somebody. But not John. The cool air soothed the throbbing in his head.

He wondered how he would tell Will that he would be leaving home soon. Although there was a sizeable age difference between them, one would be hard-pressed to find two closer brothers.

John smiled as he recalled the first time his parents invited him into the room, about an hour after William was born. He thought he would never see an uglier baby; he was almost afraid to touch him. But the moment his father cornered him, made him sit in the chair and plopped that shriveled up bundle in his lap, and Will grasped his finger, he knew he had just met his best friend.

John carelessly kicked over a bucket; it clanged against the tree, startling Will back to earth.

He glanced up, surprised to find John there.

Will ran to him and met him with that boyish grin – the grin that usually got him anything he wanted. "John, will you take me to the carnival next week? We had such fun last year! Everybody will be going."

John hesitated, meeting eyes with his little brother, inhaled a sizeable breath and spoke. "Will, I won't be here next week."

Will's face drooped. He stared back at John, struggling to understand what he was trying to tell him.

"Will, I have reached manhood – it's time for me to venture out on my own. I am going to Cleveland, Ohio."

Disappointed, Will sat down on the damp top step of the back porch.

"Cleveland? Will you take me along with you?"

John didn't know what to say, but he finally said, "My dream is to travel the world – the Great Lakes; and the sea. And Will - you will soon have a dream of your own."

Will grinned up at his big brother. "I already have one, John. I will go to the stars!"

John thought about cautioning him not to set his sights on the impossible, but he thought better of it. It would serve no good purpose to put a damper on Will's ambitions and dreams. His own dreams were ridiculed at one time, but now he was being given the opportunity to make them come true. He dropped onto the step beside Will and faced him, with a light in his eyes.

"I will be working on a river barge, Will."

Will was awestruck. "A river barge?" He jumped up - any prior signs of sadness disappeared from his tone. "That is grand! It will be the Great Adventure, John!"

John scruffed up Will's hair a little, as they walked across the back porch. "You know, father would be so proud of you, Will. You are turning out to be quite a fine young man." He pulled on the screen door handle to the kitchen. Once inside, they both stopped and slowly gave each other a sideways glance, as if positioning themselves for a race.

Their mother laughed. "I honestly don't know what I will do without the silly nightly ritual between my boys, after you've gone, John." She sighed. "You keep me young."

Soon, all that could be heard was the sound of feet, scrambling, to see who would reach the pantry door first; who would get the first cookie.

Just before he closed his eyes and drifted off to sleep, Will said, "Promise me we will always be best friends? And you won't forget me?"

"Best friends forever; I promise." John whispered as he tucked the blanket in around his baby brother. "And nothing will ever come between us."

William frowned in disappointment. "I have only one week to find you a going away present."

John smiled and shook his head as he reached to turn down the lantern. He walked slowly to the door, but he halted when he heard William whistling a little tune to himself.

"Will, would you just stop that confounded whistl …" He froze and smirked before he could finish the sentence. John stared at the floorboards between his shoes, then he did a slow turn and faced the boy in the bed.

"How about you teach me to whistle before I go away? You know I have never been able to whistle."

William responded with a wide grin. John had his answer.

And one of his gifts.

*~ Two ~*

THE NEW DAY DAWNED, overcast with a blanket of fog that hung heavy over the harvested fields.

The first of September had arrived. John sat on the bed after he finished packing his suitcase. He looked around his room – the place he had called home for as long as he remembered.

There was a map of the world on the wall opposite the doorway. Marked in red were the places he wanted to visit. John traced the lines with his finger.

As John hoisted his suitcase onto the wagon, his eyes searched high and low. But Will was nowhere to be found.

"Mother?" John said as he approached her on the back porch. "Have you seen Will? I haven't seen him since breakfast."

She began walking faster toward him. "No, I thought he was with you, John."

With worry etching his face, John leaped around the wagon and began calling out his name. "Will … Will?" He bounced and darted back and forth between the house and outbuildings, in a state of panic. He flung open the gate, nearly tearing it from its hinges and made a beeline for the barn.

As he crossed the yard, he noticed his mother at the door of the barn. He wasn't sure how long she had been standing there; he had been so upset that he hadn't paid attention to anything other than where his little brother could be. Amid the sounds of tapping and banging, she stood aside, making a formal gesture at the door, encouraging John to go inside.

Along the south wall, Will was sitting at the workbench; the workbench their father had handcrafted for the boys the summer before his death. It had been a source of delight for both boys over the last few years, even though William was only six at the time, providing an extra means to encourage them to bond and to work together.

His mother smiled as John pushed the door open.

Will was deep in concentration mode. He wore their father's canvas apron, ill-fitting as it was. John couldn't help imagining their father sitting there; helping him put the finishing touches on whatever this new project of Will's was.

"He's been at it all night," his mother said, joining her sons at the bench, as John studied the object on the table. Will carefully eased it out of the vise.

He stood and faced John, beaming from ear-to-ear. A small-headed hammer stuck out from the front pocket of the apron. After giving it further thought, he quickly whisked it behind his back and held it there with a proud smile.

John crossed his arms over his chest, pretending to be annoyed. "I was worried silly about you." Then, in a softer tone, he asked him, "What have you got there, Will?" He held out his hands.

Will waited until he was face-to-face with John – then he brought it around and placed it in his hands. John held it up, the dusty morning light streaming in through the window, pivoting and turning it so he could study it.

John smiled.

It was a star - a large, lopsided star, consisting of thin strips of hand-split hardwood, held together with square wooden pegs.

John was overwhelmed. "Will - Did you make this by yourself?"

Will nodded and grinned up at his brother. "It's a star – I made it for you."

18

~ *Three* ~

*May, 1904*

HIS THROAT CONSTRICTED as he sat in the waiting room to Lucas Camden's office. Although it wasn't the first time he had been summoned to Mr. Camden's office at the shipyard, it still set his nerves on edge.

As he had done nearly every afternoon for the past thirteen years, Lucas Camden poured himself two fingers of whiskey. He stood at the window behind his desk and drank a toast to his beloved wife, who had been gone for as many years.

Removing a thickly rolled Cuban cigar from the box, he snipped the end and struck a match to light it. He puffed until the end glowed a blazing red, with smoke trails rising toward the ceiling.

The door opened and Mr. Camden's secretary led John into the room. He studied the brass and marble nameplate sitting at the front of the desk:

*Lucas Camden – President.*

Camden folded his hands on the desk and flashed a smile as John stood at attention. "Stockton, have a seat – please."

John slowly dropped into a chair across from the desk. He swallowed hard. The twinge of anxiety ratcheted higher as the man peered up at him over his spectacles.

Camden took a deep breath. "I am an old man, John."

"Age is only a number, sir."

The tip of his cigar flared orange as he inhaled. "Then mine is 79."

"Sir, I beg your pardon, but do you think smoking is wise for you?"

A curl of blue haze writhed above his head, dissipated by the breeze from the open window. He smiled. "Actually, I find it quite amusing that these things haven't killed me yet." He walked around the front of the desk and leaned his backside against the edge. "I'm not a man who beats around the bush. I like you, John. You have a good head on your shoulders."

The cigar returned to his lips. Enveloped in another billowing gray cloud, he went on. "You've been with us for nearly four years now, haven't you?"

John nodded. "Yes sir. Three and three-quarters, to be exact, Mr. Camden."

"I am putting you in charge of the day-to-day operations at the shipyard."

"But what of your family? You have a son-in-law."

"He has no interest in shipping. He will be heading up the London division of his own father's business. My daughter has him convinced that the shipping business will never be lucrative enough to keep them happy." He pointed his cigar at John, the smoke sending John into a ripple of coughing. He apologized. "Sorry, Stockton."

Mr. Camden fiddled with one of his fancy cufflinks while he challenged him to a staring match. Then he smiled at John as he put out the cigar in the ashtray. "There's more to this that I haven't told you."

John's eyebrows arched curiously.

"My lifelong dream is about to come to fruition. Operations at Camden Enterprises will be expanding and I need your help." He motioned to John as he opened the door and handed him a set of keys. "I want you to come with me – I have something to show you."

The carriage dropped them off at the harbor.

From the outside, the waterfront property looked like a huge, long-abandoned, run-down warehouse. But as John walked through, inspecting the inside, all his mind processed was the picture-perfect place for a new shipyard. Timeworn cypress boards beneath his feet creaked and groaned, but it was music to his ears. Lucas lit another cigar and inhaled.

John was torn between the excitement of the challenge and the fear of the unknown. Camden studied John's body language from across the room. He walked briskly toward John, fresh cigar smoke trailing behind him.

"Relax, Stockton - I intend to continue to work alongside you for awhile."

~ *Four* ~

*June, 1904*

JOHN STOCKTON RETURNED to Chicago from Cleveland, to
join the small celebration as William graduated from school.

Financially assisting his mother, who had become ill, he had a
larger house built on the family plot of land; John Stockton was one of
the reasons Will had been able to stay in school, hiring a hand to help
with the farm, allowing Will the time for his academic studies.

After supper, on the first night of his weeklong visit home, John
found himself resting against a tree out back by the barn. He closed his
eyes.

"Tonight the moon is dark and the constellations are out."

John opened his eyes to find Will in front of him, holding a horse
blanket.

William walked away from the building and stood. He dropped the
blanket on the grass and kicked open the folds with his foot. John stood
and joined his brother, still in awe of the little boy who no longer
needed suspenders to hold up his britches.

Will fell backward, folding his hands across his chest, and
continued. "On nights like this, I lie out here and look up at the stars."
He went on. "It's the greatest show on Earth." He gestured for John to
join him.

William and John lay back on the blanket, looking up at a spray of stars scattered across the sky.

"See that one?" Will asked, pointing to a cluster of stars in the southern sky. "That's Centaurus. It represents the centaur."

"The centaur?"

"In Greek mythology, there is a creature that's half-horse, half man, called the centaur."

The cold prickles of grass tickled John's skin as he looked up at the sky. "I do remember something like that from the books back in school. Those Greeks sure had some crazy imaginations – doesn't look like a half-horse, half-man to me."

Will continued wistfully staring at the sky as if he hadn't heard anything John said.

John laughed a little, and then he turned to face Will, with a blaze in his eyes. "There are so many opportunities out there for you, Will – things I will never be able to accomplish."

Will stiffened. His eyes turned away from John.

"This is just the beginning," John continued. "You have so much life ahead of you. First college, then …" But William didn't let him finish. He rolled over to look his big brother in the eye. Then he blew out a frustrated breath and quickly jumped up.

John chuckled. "Chiggers, Will? Do you remember the time we both returned home covered in them? Poor mother; she had such a time ridding us of them, didn't she?"

With his back to his brother, Will drew in a long breath and he spoke. "It's not chiggers, John."

John looked at him sideways, with a puzzled expression. Then after a few moments of silence, he inquired, "Then what?"

William placed his hands in his pants pockets and he shrugged. "It's nothing."

John added, "That didn't work when you were six and it still doesn't work. Why do I feel like I'm racing to catch up with a runaway train? What's bothering you, Will?"

"I don't intend to go on to college here."

"*What?*" He raised his voice. "*Good God,* Will! You have been accepted at Yale University! Have you completely lost your mind?" Do you understand what you will be giving up?"

Will slapped at a mosquito on his neck. "John, I know that you want me to attend Yale, and that you have made it possible …"

"Will - no amount of money could have gotten you an entrance ticket to Yale, if you hadn't already proven yourself worthy through your academic intelligence and unquenchable thirst for knowledge."

"But, John, - *that's just it!* "He dropped back to the blanket, rolled over, propping himself up on his elbows. He met his big brother's eyes with a fiery blaze that paralyzed John. "For my part I know nothing with any certainty, but the sight of the stars makes me dream."

John studied Will's face. "I don't know what you just said, but it sounds complicated."

"Van Gogh."

"Who?"

"Vincent Van Gogh. He said that." Then he bounced back to his feet. Will looked up at the sky and spoke again, framing his words carefully. "Do you think it will ever be possible to travel to the moon; and the stars, John?" John opened his mouth to answer, but William didn't let him – he jumped back in with, "Well I do ... and I want to be there when it happens." He held out a small bundle to John; something wrapped in a thin, cotton veil. "This was given to me by Robert Spencer."

John's eyebrows arched as he revealed a small, hand-held telescope. "Mr. Spencer from the school board?" John held it up to view the night sky.

Will nodded and added, "He also gave this to me."

John stared at him, speechless. William unfolded a brochure he had tucked into his back pocket. He handed it to John.

"Dublin?" John asked him. *"The one in Ireland?"*

~ *Five* ~

*January, 1908*

THE GROUP OF YOUNG WOMEN were staring at him from the front porch, drooling as he passed them by on his way to the docks. He tipped his hat and offered a charming grin. He looked at the group again and did a double take. "Good morning, ladies."

John had never worked so physically hard in his life. He'd thought working on the family farm had made him stronger, fitter, but ripping out old warped boards, prying off and taking down thousands of rotting shakes, dragging loads of junk and debris to the salvage yards, was a whole different kind of workout.

Still it was progress. Every shingle, every warped board he hauled out of there was one step closer to the time when they would be able to start the real renovation; start making Camden's plans come to life.

He had been manager of the new shipyard for almost four years when John received a message that he was being called to Mr. Camden's home.

The illness had aged Camden at least a decade in a mere four years. More and more, the shipping magnate had withdrawn himself from public life, retreating to his estate on the southern edge of Cleveland. By the time he had met with his attorneys, he had fallen so weak that he required round-the-clock care.

John sat quietly by his mentor's side and watched the life slowly drain from the old man.

The nurse entered the room and touched John's shoulder. "Mr. Camden is tiring. He needs his rest …"

But Lucas interrupted her with a sound that was something between a laugh and a cough. Then he reached out in John's direction. "Stockton, give me your hand." John gave the nurse a questioning look, but she nodded. He took Camden's hand.

"John, I have had all the legal documents drawn up and I've signed everything. But the most important part comes now - the handshake; the human touch." He inhaled and exhaled a cough. "The future - it belongs to you; the young … the inspired."

John tightened his grip on the man's bony hand.

"The world is full of skeptics," he told John. "I know – I'm one myself. But you can be successful and still be a good human being."

John's eyes shifted downward.

"Stockton – make no mistake," Lucas breathed with the slightest touch of steel in his voice, "although I have the utmost confidence and faith in your abilities …" Camden's gaze met John's, "It will be hard work."

"Sir, I will make it my life's ambition to continue your financial success."

Camden shot up so quickly that his oil lamp tipped over, clattering onto the floor. His eyes glittered with a fierce emotion that John couldn't place. Aggravation? Rage? Whatever it was, it was frightening.

John quickly picked up the lamp and placed it back on the table at his side. Then Lucas relaxed and leaned back in the bed. He reached for John's hand again. He attempted to speak, but he could only offer a whisper. John leaned in as the old man breathed,

"Strive not to be a success, but rather to be of value. Never forget the human touch." John smiled at him and nodded.

"Thank you Mr. Camden."

"The world is hastily evolving, son. But never forget …" He turned slightly and looked at the lamp again. "No incandescent electric bulb will ever compete with the warmth and beauty of candle flame."

Lucas Camden died and left the business to John in his will, much to his daughter's chagrin. Nevertheless, it was solid – John was truly the son Camden never had.

~ *Six* ~

*June, 1911*

THE WAGON CARRYING JOHN pulled into the yard. He took in the view and beamed.

William had moved to Ireland permanently after graduating early, with honors, from Dublin University.

Over the next few years, the two brothers had become so busy with their own lives that they only communicated my mail, with the exception of the passing of their mother. John had moved her to Cleveland, to care for her during her final weeks. Will made it back in time to see her before she passed, but he couldn't stay long – the observatory needed him to function, so he returned to Ireland the day following her funeral service.

As fate would have it, John had a block of time – almost two months after the day of the funeral, at the end of June. He was eager to see, for himself, the life William had chosen over joining him in the shipping business.

John had immersed himself in the company, allowing no time-off for recreation or a real social life. He had little time for himself – his adult life had consisted mainly of work and travel. So the idea of a month-long holiday in Ireland, with no responsibilities, greatly appealed to him.

And he looked forward to spending time with William on an occasion other than a funeral.

It was an old stone farmhouse, surrounded by lush land and mature trees. There was a little well-tended garden surrounding it. The patch overlooked a bank of rocks. Beyond that was an uneven coastline and then the aqua-blue sea. He was beginning to understand why his baby brother chose to remain in Ireland instead of returning to the states.

After John had gotten unpacked and settled in, William led him down a footpath to an old wooden bridge, and through the woods for about a half mile.

It took John a moment to untangle Will's words as he chattered blissfully about his new home.

"So, do you think you are up to a hike?" he asked his big brother.

John grinned back at him and replied, "I believe I am up to the challenge, Will."

After what seemed like they had walked on an incline for miles, they reached the top. John stopped and inhaled deeply. Then he exhaled.

Countless acres of green in every imaginable shade and texture rolled out below them.

"It takes my breath away," Will said with a smile.

"I understand – I find myself breathless as well."

⁎⁎⁎⁑⁎⁑⁎⁎⁎⁑⁎⁑⁎⁎

Will settled onto a stool at the bar and proudly introduced his sibling to the inhabitants of Quinn's Harbor.

The Stockton boys each ordered a pint at O'Brien's Pub to occupy their time while they waited for their sandwiches to arrive.

"Will, the two of you could be twins, you look so alike," Michael, the bartender remarked." He dried a mug and placed it on the shelf behind him. "How many years apart did you say the two of you were?"

Will chuckled. "Nearly nine years." John opened his mouth to make a joke, but before he could say anything, Will jumped back in with, "That must be because I am much worldlier than my 23 years."

Everybody laughed.

A big-bellied man rose from a corner table and approached them from behind. "Your brother, Will here, holds the Quinn's Harbor title for whistling," he said, slapping a hand across John's back.

The corner of John's eyes crinkled. "Is that so?"

"Another pint for each of my good friends here," the man shouted out, gesturing for the bartender.

When Michael returned, fists full of ale, the man leaned in and just before he returned to his table, added, "Now, don't be thinkin' of taking our Will back to America with you." He winked. "We aren't about to give him up without a good fight."

"I can see that." John replied, with a laugh, just before his lips reached the rim of his mug.

When Michael was called to the kitchen, William became pensive - preoccupied.

John leaned in. "Is something bothering you, Will? I've known you for all of those 23 years, and I think I can tell when you've got something on your mind."

Will leaned in as well, sliding his mug around on the table between his hands. "Well John, since you brought up the subject, I do have something I want to discuss with you."

John put down his mug and wiped his mouth with his shirtsleeve.

His little brother looked him square in the eyes. He drew in such a deep breath that John expected the half-full mugs on their table to shift a little towards him. "John, I have taken a fancy to a young woman from Quinn's Harbor."

John shot him a *knowing* grin, but Will held up his hand. "This is not just any girl, John." He took a deep swig from his mug, polishing it off.

Michael happened to be passing by, noticing Will's empty mug. His towel circled the glass in his hand and he set it on the bar. "Two more, boys?"

John nodded. He felt a manhood milestone fast approaching. "This round is on me, Michael."

"John, I don't pretend to know how to impress a woman like this. You know I have courted more than one girl in my lifetime, but this one is different. Every time I open my mouth to speak, no words come out."

"You are so worldly with women. What is a man to do? How can I let her know my intentions?" Two pints appeared in front of them, on the table.

John smiled. "Does she have a name?" he asked.

Will leaned in and whispered, "I don't want to reveal her identity yet, John – this is a very small community."

John smiled. As a young man, John's fancy was caught often. But never for long. Patrons of the pub leaned toward them, hoping to catch a morsel of Will's older brother's advice; advice about how Americans won their women over.

"Will - the way into a woman's heart is this: You must play hard –to-get, even if it appears that you are ignoring her. Believe me - that will attract her all the more to you." John was proud, pleased to pass along this Stockton pearl of wisdom - *rite of passage,* to his sibling.

"But John, I cannot give her the impression that I don't like her – that sounds like it could backfire and I could lose any chance I have." Will tipped back his mug and polished off his third pint. "I've spoken to her casually from time to time. She seems to like me; we even shared a dance last month at the old school dance, in town.

"Even better," John quipped. "She already likes you – you're halfway to the finish line."

William laughed a little at that and his eyes warmed as he continued on about the girl.

Later, a bit overserved, they stumbled their way back to the house, John singing while William whistled, providing the background music.

After the third refrain, Will stopped and faced John. "Now, I'll sing and *you* whistle." But John didn't reply.

Then it hit him. Could it be? Will faced his big brother and hiccupped, his eyes wide. "John! Don't tell me - you *still* can't whistle?"

~ *Seven* ~

THE FOLLOWING MORNING, John rose early and set out for a walk.

Although he possessed a keen sense of direction, and his lucky compass in his pocket, Captain Stockton found himself turned around and unable to find the same beautiful spot William had taken him to. Not to worry though, because the countryside had a wealth of alternate places to admire and take in God's work.

After a few hours, John found a comfy spot against an old Oak tree, near an irresistible view of a river, just past a weathered sign that read, *Quinn's Harbor*.

Quinn's Harbor's rugged beauty reminded him of his boyhood home. After situating himself along the waterfront, a mile from town, his mind wandered off to the whistling melody of the dancing water. And he faded.

✫✫✫✫✫✫✫✫✫✫✫✫

The early afternoon sunlight streaked across his face, gently waking him from the reverie of suspended animation. John yawned lazily and stood. The light sent a soft shimmer across the landscape, making it appear like a scene from a dream.

He felt her before he saw her. His eyes focused on movement across the river. He paused.

A line that had been pulled tightly between two Alder trees danced joyfully in the breeze with an array of freshly laundered clothing.

She appeared to be much younger than his own 32 years; she mesmerized him – he found it impossible to tear his eyes away from her.

The woman unbuttoned her shoes and pulled off her stockings before placing them neatly on the rocky shore. John quickly stepped behind a tree and looked away just as she turned to face the river, fearing he might frighten her. He observed from a distance as she waded in the shallow end of the river.

Then, shifting restlessly, she took a glance up and down the river, found nobody there, and impulsively shed her skirt and shirtwaist, keeping on only her undergarments. She carelessly tossed everything onto the rocks, in a gleeful gesture of absolute freedom.

*What spirit!*

She removed the combs from her hair, setting her locks free to fall over her shoulders. He memorized her profile, her curves, and the swell that rose over the bodice of her corset.

She waded into the river, then floated to deeper water, where she dove in, only to resurface again, her wet hair slicked back, accentuating a set of beautiful eyes.

John felt a tinge of guilt, staring; spying on the striking young woman; she was certainly entitled to her privacy. And he had always prided himself on being a gentleman, although the string of admiring young women he took out in the evenings had presented him with many opportunities over the years to prove otherwise. A gentleman, yes, but he was also known for being an absolute flirt.

He frowned and reluctantly turned and began to continue along on his walk.

A strong, hasty breeze enveloped the riverbank; the young woman squinted over just in time to watch her skirt and blouse rolling across the rocks, like tumbleweed in the wind, toward the water.

John heard a shriek from behind him and dashed back to the riverfront, where he observed her skirt and shirtwaist as they tumbled closer and closer to the river's edge. He lunged forward and snagged the skirt seconds before it reached the cliff.

He rushed to continue on his mission. John made every effort to detain the blouse as well, but it escaped and proceeded over the edge, landing gracefully on the water before disappearing completely beneath its surface.

She saw him walking toward the riverbank, holding her skirt. His clothes fit him so perfectly, his hair impeccably groomed, that he could have been going to a dinner party. She squinted up at him, while treading water, as if the sun's glare was too intense.

He grinned. "There's nothing like plunging into cold water on a hot day."

"Sir, would you be so kind as to hand me my skirt?"

The unstable dirt and rocks collapsed beneath his feet, and he slid on his heels toward the riverbank, catching himself on a branch. He inched slowly toward the water with her skirt, his feet clipping and sliding over the algae-covered stones.

He stopped on the rocky ledge, just above where she was treading water. John leaned in and relinquished the skirt to her outstretched hand. She quickly snatched it from his grip.

He looked down at her, with a teasing smile. "Mind if I ask how you plan to go about putting your skirt on underwater?" He offered her his hand. "Perhaps I might be able to assist you ..."

"I assure you, sir, that I am quite capable of many things." She continued to tread the current as best she could with one free hand; she lifted her chin above the water, bobbing up and down. She tried to chuckle a little, but her distress was becoming obvious to John.

"You'd best be turning around and give a lass some privacy," she went on, in a delicate Irish brogue.

John turned around and continued to converse with her, but after a few moments, she stopped talking. He quickly spun around.

She was nowhere in sight. He swiftly searched the river for some sign of the woman. His heart sped up. Finally, he spotted the skirt swirling just under the water's surface.

John had become quite proficient in the art of swimming, having found himself thrown overboard on many occasions while sailing during inclement weather, so the question never entered his mind. He kicked off his boots, threw off his jacket and shirt, then he dove into the river after her.

Slapping at the water as she attempted to resurface, she fought to keep her head above water.

"Swim toward me if you can!" John directed, his voice loud and firm.

She appeared to be struggling in such a panic, it left little doubt in John's mind that she was caught up in her skirt, fighting for her life. The water rippled in circles around her and she began sinking again.

Swimming with long, steady strokes, he glanced up, but didn't immediately see her. The current crashed over his face, obscuring his vision.

The young woman had disappeared, hidden by a sharply jutting rock. Then he caught sight of her as she bobbed up for air. All he needed was to be able to get close enough; a few strong thrusts. He had just gotten hold of her when she suddenly dropped under the water's surface again.

John was expecting her to fight him, and she did at first, but she suddenly collapsed against him as he pulled on the lacing running up the back of her corset. She had passed out, making it easier for him to hold her.

He sliced through the water with the grace and ease of an athlete as he swam toward the riverbank. Once safely ashore, John carried her away from the riverbank.

## ~ Eight ~

WHEN SHE OPENED HER EYES, there were two pools of stormy water looking back at her. For a moment, she wondered if she was drowning again.

The afternoon sunlight glinted off his bare upper body. His hair fell in wet, unruly strands over his forehead. Beads of moisture dripped from his skin as he carried her and gently rested her limp body in a soft, grassy area, just beyond the shale bed.

John's eyes peered down at her from beneath a fringe of heavy eyelashes. He studied her eyes; her cheekbones. He became aware of the slight paleness of her skin where her blouse had protected her from the sun. She looked fragile.

Her hair was tangled and wet, the strands in the front clinging to her face. She struggled to sit up. He leaned over and stared down at her; her skin turned warm and pink.

His eyes squinted as he smiled. "Well now - you gave me quite a scare for a moment back there."

As she raised up, her eyes dropped to her body. She felt completely exposed, out there in her wet underclothes, on display for all to see.

John stood and picked up his jacket, shirt and boots from the overhang. He noticed the heel on one of his boots had been knocked out of alignment – a thought he quickly dismissed as he gathered her shoes and stockings. He returned to her side.

She tried to stand on her own, but John reached out and steadied her as she swayed. Concern etched his brow. He couldn't ignore the way she had her arms wrapped around herself and how hard she was shivering.

"Easy now." John rubbed her arms. "You are chilled to the bone."

The lass shivered in the gentle breeze. "I'm fine." She clenched her teeth together to silence the chattering.

*Minus the wooziness in my head.* She shivered continuously as he wrapped her in the warmth of his coat.

Blushing from her eyebrows to her ankles, she knew it wasn't just from embarrassment - much of it was from attraction – more than she was familiar with. He had to have felt the invasion of goosebumps that rose over her arms at his touch.

"I must look frightful," referring to the tangled mass of strands that had worked their way loose and were now hanging over her eyes.

He plucked a twig from her hair. "Allow me," he said, gently tucking the stray tresses behind her ears. His smile transformed the seemingly simple act into something incredibly intimate; her cheeks reddened. He helped her to her feet.

"Mind your head," John instructed her as he pushed a low Alder branch out of the way and held it up for her, like a doorman holding open a door. He handed her the driest article of clothing from the line – a cotton print housedress.

*Naturally, it would be the most unattractive thing hanging on the clothesline.*

She held it up in front of her, as if to be sizing up the garment. She glared over at the stranger and quipped, "Well, are you going to just stand there and watch me, or are you going to turn around?"

A flush slid through his cheeks. With a mischievous glint in his eyes, he added, "My dear, you haven't left much to the imagination as it is." Then he winked at her.

She blushed. Then John turned around.

While she was changing, John gathered the remaining clothes from the line, and set them in her basket.

Once she was confident enough that she was fully clothed, although she wasn't happy that there was no mirror in sight, she spoke. "There. I think I am appropriately dressed to be in the company of a gentleman now."

When John turned around, he almost choked on his own saliva, squelching the urge to laugh at the sight of how ill-fitting his selection from the clothesline was. The gaping armholes extended down past her hips, meeting the hemline in places, creating the image of an amusing, lopsided cartoon character from the newspapers.

When she caught the humor in his eyes, she giggled. "My aunt is much shorter than I am." He picked up the basket as she gathered the dress in the front with her hands and began walking along, following the path with him.

He felt a flash of humor. "And although I have never met her, I believe your aunt might be a little on the portly side." He gave her a sideways smile.

At the edge of the riverbank, where the road went in different directions, the woman stopped and smiled up at John – a smile that was contagious. "This is where I must turn off – I live a bit down this road."

John set the willow basket onto the dusty path. There was a moment of awkward silence, but the smile they shared between them tempered it.

"And I thank you. Perhaps we will meet again." She balanced the willow basket on one side, grabbed a fist full of her aunt's dress with her other hand and smiled back at him. She looked ridiculous, but he really didn't notice.

She turned and continued on her way; he gave her a wave.

*With any luck, we most certainly will meet again, if I have anything to say about it.*

The route back to his brother's house ran parallel to the riverbank. He paused at the western edge of the water, deep in thought.

John found himself unable to think clearly. All he could see in his head was the vision of the young woman in her thin, wet undergarments. He just stood there on the rocks, smiling like an idiot. This was unusual behavior for him.

Not only that – it was downright frightening.

# ~ *Nine* ~

JOHN CHUCKLED TO HIMSELF, as the third person in town that morning mistook him for his younger sibling.

"Mornin' Will," the man sporting the handlebar moustache greeted him, with a tip of his hat.

An older gentleman elbowed the first man as John passed them. "That's not Will, Mr. O'Toole - that's the young man's older sibling."

The first man stroked the edges of his moustache and smiled. He nodded. "Aye – Whistler's Brother."

From that point on, the name stuck.

Just before he turned in for the evening, Will stood back from the stairs, signaling John that he wanted to talk to him.

"Are you quite sure I am doing the right thing – paying no attention to the woman?" His mind was in a state of turmoil.

John slowly nodded his head in affirmation. He closed his journal and stood. "A man needs to establish control of the relationship, at the very start, if it is to become a lasting one."

Will raised his eyebrows. "But what if —"

John jumped in, heading him off at the pass. "Above all Will, I must stress the importance of steering the relationship so that you maintain control at all times." Then, with a knowing grin, he went on. "By the time you are ready, she will not be able to resist you."

"Very well, John. I will stay on this path."

Will got up and walked to the doorway. He clearly wanted to say something else, but he thought better of it and continued up the stairs. After all, John had his best interest at heart; he would have no reason to send him in the wrong direction.

## ~ *Ten* ~

A FEW DAYS LATER, John set off to town to the shoemaker to have the heel of his boot repaired. He dropped off the boot and headed out the door into the street toward Dalton's Bakery.

"Are you sure you don't want them delivered?"

"No thank you," she assured Mr. Dalton. Her need to prove her independence did her more harm than good at times. She awkwardly tucked the parcels under her chin and arm, carefully balancing the others. She yanked on the handle and walked briskly out the door of the bakery – straight into John Stockton's arms.

The feel of the young woman, leaning into him as she struggled to keep a loaf of bread from falling, while holding onto two bags and a basket of fruit, disoriented John for a glorious moment.

He fumbled to regain his balance while making sure she was steady. She laughed nervously, gripping his arm as she watched her parcels fall to the street.

He felt a flash of recognition. *It's her.*

John tipped his hat to the back of his head and grinned. "Fancy meeting you here. Remember me? I'm John."

He did something to her stomach, or maybe it was her heart; she couldn't help herself. "Katie." She grinned back at him with a mock curtsy.

"Pleasure to meet you, Katie." His hand brushed hers as he took the basket from her, and he let his fingers linger a little longer than necessary.

John assisted her in gathering her packages, inspecting them each for damage. He held up the broken loaf of bread in front of his face and wrinkled his nose. "I think this bread has seen better days."

She giggled. Her inquisitive eyes sparkled. "I am certain you are not from around here. Let me guess … America?"

He nodded and inhaled deeply. "It doesn't matter where you're from - there's nothing better than the smell of freshly-baked bread."

They headed back into the bakery together.

John drew in with a blissful sigh. "See? Does anything smell better than this?"

Katie and John both found it intriguing that neither one questioned why they instinctively continued on the shopping excursion together – it just felt right.

John stopped in front of Maguire's Market. Katie grinned. "Maguire's has the freshest produce anywhere."

John browsed through the market, adding berries and peaches to his basket, when it became evident to him that the people working at the market knew Katie well - they all called her by name.

"The market belongs to my Aunt Rose." She placed three pears in his basket, and added, "You'll be wanting these too, I'm sure."

*I am fairly sure I am looking at something else I want, even more than pears.*

"I work in the market myself, four days out of the week – I have since the day I turned fourteen."

John made his purchase, while Katie ventured across the way to a cheese vendor. John caught up with her while she was visiting with a young man wearing a tan apron, holding a half-wedge of cheddar.

She introduced the two. "John - this is Tyler. We've known each other since we were little babes, in diapers." John noticed that the young man she was talking to was very attentive to her.

"And Tyler; meet John. He's from America."

They shook hands.

John smiled, but was surprised to feel a little tinge of jealousy. Shrugging it off, he continued walking with Katie toward the edge of town, carrying half of her parcels for her.

He watched her juggle the bags from one side to the other. "You have so much to carry. I hope you will permit me to deliver these home for you."

She allowed him to take them, while thinking to herself.

*I hope he doesn't remember that I had no trouble carrying the laundry basket, which was much heavier.*

Simultaneously, John's thoughts carried on.

*I hope she doesn't remind me that these packages are far less cumbersome than the laundry she carried home a few days ago.*

There was a shady area, perfect for a picnic, just beyond the sign for Quinn's Harbor. They sat for awhile, to counteract the hot weather.

Katie encouraged John to try a bite of cheese – a special variety he had never tried before.

As he took a bite of the cheese, Katie commented on how her Aunt's produce stand was the largest and had the freshest produce in Ireland.

He grinned. "Yes, it is certainly something to be proud of."

"Do you have many markets back home where you live?"

John nodded. He couldn't help thinking that Maguire's paled in comparison to the market that was being constructed just around the corner from where he lived, on the near west side of Cleveland. Scheduled to open in less than a year, he described it to her.

"And when it's finished, it's going to be grand."

"How grand?" she asked.

He looked her in the eyes. "There will be over a hundred shops. And I hear it's going to have a clock tower, over a hundred and thirty foot tall."

It all sounded too good to be true to Katie. She widened her eyes. After a moment, she decided she didn't believe him.

*The man is pulling my leg.*

"Blarney." She hooted a laugh and fell back on the soft, green turf.

He uprooted a blade of grass, rubbed it between his palms and pretended to look offended.

"You don't believe me? Aren't you being a little hard on me? I have a reputation for being quite honest, I'll have you know, but you seem to take great delight in mocking me."

"Perhaps that's because somebody needs to."

John sat back, but only for a moment. He moved closer to her, brushing her hand, making her dizzy just by his presence.

Katie wondered how many hearts he had broken. She stared down at their hands, almost touching.

John bent his head, lower and lower, until he invaded Katie's line of vision and she had no choice but to meet his eyes. The most enchanting smudges of pink blossomed on her cheeks as he studied her through irresistible, thick eyelashes. He was delighted.

He found himself fascinated by her intensity and wit; her curiosity and laughter charmed him. And he wanted more.

After they had walked for another fifteen minutes, the road changed from gravel-covered dirt to just dirt.

The sun slid behind a cloud as they paused at the same fork in the road as the previous time. She looked up at John and smiled. "My house is just a bit down the road, this way." She pointed and smiled as he followed her. "I will only keep you a few more moments."

John delivered the parcels and Katie safely home - far sooner than he wanted to. The cottage was an old stone-built structure with a tiled roof and whitewashed walls, perched on a rocky cliff above the shore. Flowers bloomed in a wooden box, directly under a little second-story window.

Katie watched John's eyes shift to the window. She beamed. "That's my bedroom."

"It must be quite a small room." John smiled at her in a teasing manner.

"Oh, but I love it. The very first night I spent here, in Quinn's Harbor, I couldn't sleep." She turned to John and explained further. "My mother died when I was just a wee lass and Rose took me in."

His smile faded. "I'm sorry, Katie. I didn't know."

Katie pointed up at the window. She went on. "And my aunt took me up to the attic and sat with me in front of that very window." She folded her hands and placed them beneath her chin. "First we watched the lights out on the harbor - counting them, like little stars, while we ate biscuits."

John touched Katie's elbow and studied the wistful look in her eyes as she continued. "Then she told me a story about a little girl who found a magic place where she could see everything and everybody she desired; she was never truly alone in the attic."

Katie stepped up onto the porch. John, still holding her arm, went with her. She smiled. "It took me awhile, but I finally realized that the magic was not in the attic itself, but in the *belief* that the room possessed magical powers."

He moved the bags on the porch, closer to the door. Looking her deep in the eyes, he said, "Goodbye Katie. I shall be watching for you again, soon."

John's heart teetered closer and closer to the edge. He leaned in and kissed her; a quick peck on the cheek, but it was a start.

She smiled at him and the sun came out.

John had not been interested in the complication of a romance. However, he had to admit, he was taken by her - by the fact that she had no idea anyone could be taken by her. And he had no clue what to do about it.

That was when John began to realize just how deep in trouble he actually was.

## ~ *Eleven* ~

THE BOYS REACHED the shore at the crack of dawn. They shoved the rowboat off the sand and hopped in. Will pushed them out into the water using the paddle for leverage, then he faced John.

"John, I've drafted a letter; a letter outlining my intentions." Will held out a folded paper for John to read.

"It's too soon, Will." He shook his head slowly and pushed the note back to him.

Will gave him a look of sheer agony.

His tone was even and calm; they'd had this conversation before. One corner of John's mouth lifted up in a smile. "Just a bit more time, and she will be yours. Trust me."

The rowboat bobbed in the water. Will grunted, but whether in agreement or dissent, John couldn't tell.

He dismissed it. "Don't fret about it. Now, let's have a look at this motor." But as John pulled the cable on the outboard, his half-smile disappeared.

*If I could only take my own advice.*

After a supper consisting of fresh trout, they went outside and sat on the back porch.

When Will's eyes turned heavenward, to begin the ritual of counting stars, he took in a breath and exhaled. "You know, I still dream about the stars every night, John. I never tire of it." He stepped off the porch and walked toward the barn. "Do you feel the same about the Great Lakes and the seas?"

His big brother followed him. "I suppose I do, Will. I never thought about it until now."

Will pulled the door to the horse barn closed and latched it.

John proudly grinned at Will. "Although I have cultivated a passion for the stars as well, thanks to you." He grinned and pointed in the sky. "Cassiopeia."

"You impress me, John. It seems you have taken an interest in astronomy."

"Oh, some 12 years ago, I was given a gift." He gave Will a half-sideways glance. He smiled. "A star." He rubbed his hand over his face and continued. "And it served as a reminder that I certainly could not allow my little brother the advantage of expertise superior to mine in any area."

Will attempted to stifle a chuckle, nearly choking.

"That was a pretty pathetic attempt at crafting a star, John. I should apologize, although it's a bit late, isn't it?" He grinned at his brother.

John stood and stared wistfully into the night sky. "That star has accompanied me on every voyage I have ever taken, Will."

## ~ Twelve ~

THE DAY WAS BRIGHT and sunny. He watched her sitting on the rocks, eating her lunch. He noticed that for every bite Katie took of her sandwich, she broke off a tiny piece of bread and tossed it to the birds. Not just once, but every time she took a bite. He was intrigued.

John was so engrossed in what she was doing, that his foot slipped on a rock as he glanced over his shoulder, the sound of snapping twigs sending the birds fluttering away in a tizzy.

She turned and spotted John, as he attempted to pick himself up off the ground. She strolled over to him with a cockeyed smile. When she got close enough, she teased him. "Well, I dare say, that's one way to make your presence known."

John stood and dusted off the seat of his trousers. A patchy breeze tugged at the hem of Katie's dress, like a child wanting to be noticed.

A quick grin flashed and his dimples winked. "I wonder if you placed those branches there to trap me?"

She widened her eyes and playfully swatted at him. John ducked away from the impish swipe. Her face cracked into a bashful smile.

He wondered if he had unintentionally offended her; that was the last thing he had wanted to do. This woman was very different than any other he had ever met, and he didn't want her to pull away from him. He wanted to see her again - good Lord, he did. He fought it but he could not bring himself to follow his own advice.

Indecision played across his handsome features. If he pretended not to be interested, she might take him seriously. Then what? He could lose his chance with her. His fingers circled her arm and didn't let go as they walked.

"Is America as thrilling as the stories we hear?" She turned and met his eyes. "What do you do there?"

He chuckled. His life was not boring, but he never thought of it as particularly exciting. "Actually, I come from a long line of farmers. Farming has been in my family for generations."

Katie smiled up at him, squinting her eyes in the sunlight.

John continued. "I am, however, in the shipbuilding business. I've been at it for seven years now."

"If shipbuilding hasn't been in your family, how did you decide that this was what you wanted to do?" Katie asked.

*She is intelligent.*

"Obviously, it was not my original idea – the industry had already been established there; shipbuilding is not the backbone of the city, but there is a need, and the setting is perfect for it. So I spend some of my time building ships and the rest of it, sailing them."

Ripples crossed her forehead. "Common sense."

A light breeze cooled his face. He gave her an inquisitive look.

"That's what I see when I look at you." Then she grinned.

He wasn't at all sure where that left him. He raised his eyebrows at the nonchalant way she'd said it. What was that supposed to mean? Was it good or bad? John touched her cheek.

The way he moved took her breath away. She liked him, but in a different way than she had ever liked any boy … any *man*. Every time she looked at him, her heart tried to escape and run for cover.

"You travel the world?"

He nodded. "I find myself on the water most of the time."

"Is that what you want, John? A life disconnected from roots?"

"Oh, I am very connected to the land. America is beautiful. But there is just something that lures me to the water. I have no ties at this time in my life, so that's how I choose to spend it." He stopped beside an old Alder tree and placed his hands on his hips.

"Well, I think I've heard enough about me. What about you, Katie? Tell me about your dreams."

She tried to look away, but John wouldn't allow it. He shifted his fingers, resting under her chin, and tilted her head upward.

Katie looked up at him, the sunlight bouncing off her hair; eyes revealing that she wasn't sure she should say it. She turned away slightly, and told him, "I would like to aid people."

"You want to be a nurse?" he asked.

"Maybe. But I really want to work to help others; to teach them how to help themselves ... so that they may live fuller lives."

She held her breath, praying that he wouldn't laugh at her. Airing out the soul posed a certain danger. It was risky to expose such deeply rooted longings and hard to guess how he would respond.

"I envy you." she heard him say, quietly.

Katie looked back to see if he was mocking her, but there was no outward expression, only a gentle sort of wistfulness. His eyes closed as he drank in the sweet scent of her skin. He moved closer to her, making her dizzy just by his presence.

Katie walked backwards until she bumped up against the trunk of a tree. A smile hovered on his mouth as he leaned in to kiss her.

It was impossibly romantic.

She kissed him back.

Katie drew in a breath as he moved even closer and wrapped his arms around her waist. Putting his finger to her lips, he softly hushed her. John lowered his head again and pressed his lips to hers, gently at first, then, as she closed her eyes and leaned in, he pulled her closer.

Tenderness and frustration wavered across his face, as if he wanted to take her in his arms and push her away at the same time.

A momentary jolt of fear slammed his confidence, but dissipated quickly. "I'll apologize, if you would like me to, he said gently." Then he added, "But I would be lying."

She yearned for him to mold himself to her, like the final missing piece of a complex jigsaw puzzle. Uncontainable thoughts continued to race through her head; wildly inappropriate notions.

Was she in love or was she embarrassed? Or both? All at once, Katie realized that she didn't have enough experience to know the difference.

*This must be lust.* She had read the word in literature, but never before had she understood what it was.

"That merry twinkle in yer eye may get you farther than you think, John." She felt the blood rush into her face when she suddenly realized how the comment could have been misinterpreted.

*Oh my - that was not how I meant it to sound.*

For a moment, John looked shocked – then his eyes twinkled; he knew what she really meant – although he would have loved it if she'd meant something entirely different.

He couldn't help staring at Katie; he felt his chest expand just looking at her. There was no point in fighting it any longer.

John was already in love with her.

## ~ Thirteen ~

THE FOLLOWING DAYS quickly transformed into weeks. John and Katie spent nearly every afternoon together, sharing their lunch at the river; sometimes lasting well into the sunset.

* * * * * * * * * * * * * *

John stepped up onto the porch and breathed in the evening air, freshly streaked with shades of purple, fuchsia and gold. Sunset had quickly become his favorite time of the day. He turned the doorknob and found William sitting at the kitchen table, looking serious.

Will's gut clenched, knowing his brother would not approve of his decision. He forced himself not to think about what could happen if he continued to follow John's guidance, possibly losing the young woman forever.

Struggling with his own situation, John had been finding it increasingly more difficult to give Will advice on women.

"I cannot wait for you to meet my girl, at the festival tomorrow, John," Will said, beaming. "I have no doubt you will be almost as smitten as I am with her."

"I'd like to talk to you, Will," John said, sounding like he was reading from a script.

Will heaved a sigh and waited for the lecture.

John continued. "I have a feeling about tomorrow night. I believe this will be the perfect time for you to tell her." He smacked his brother lightly on the back and chuckled.

The weight of the world was suddenly lifted from his shoulders. It was almost as if, by giving Will his blessing to move forward with his plan, he was releasing himself from the tension that had been building within his own soul over the last few weeks.

And perhaps now it was his own time to freely commit to the young woman who had taken his heart prisoner. Their mother always said that God sometimes had an odd way of making dreams come true.

John felt absolutely wonderful. He would be meeting Katie at the harbor later. The anticipation mounted; he could hardly contain himself. He smiled a little wider in the mirror as he ran the razor across his face – unusual to be doing this twice in one day, but it just felt right.

He wanted everything to be perfect.

## ~ Fourteen ~

IT WAS DARK, but Katie knew her way to the water's edge. She hesitated as she started up the path; there was a tiny light bouncing up and down at the far end of the footbridge, followed by boots making sharp raps on the wooden plank trestle.

She caught her breath and felt a warm blush creep across her face; she wasn't sure exactly what she was feeling. But it had everything to do with the man facing her on the bridge, less than fifty feet away.

With the flicker of the amber flame from the lantern dancing over his chiseled features, he was, without question, the handsomest man she had ever laid eyes on.

John met Katie almost dead center on the bridge. He looked at the sky above them. "I don't think we'll need the lantern tonight," he said as he put out the flame.

Moonlight guided their path through a break in the canopy of vegetation overhead to the river. He climbed the steps to the dock. Just ahead of the high season, the soon-to-be busy pier looked a little like a ghost town. John stepped up.

The deep sound of a foghorn out on the bay and a faraway soft light warned of a freighter passing through on its way out to sea. Katie jumped a little and he stepped closer, steadying her by slipping his arms around her waist. He helped her up to join him.

John gazed into her eyes. He drew in a slow breath as he pulled her close.

The moment Katie was in his arms, John closed his eyes and sighed deeply. Everything was as it should be. He inhaled the scent of her skin and her hair. He whispered against her ear. "I've waited so long for you to come into my life."

Fireflies glimmered in the scrub down by the water's edge as they eavesdropped on the conversation, begging for more.

John's hand tangled in her hair, disarranging her hairpins, as he continued to whisper, unsteadily. "You mustn't ever be afraid of me, Katie. I would sooner throw myself in front of a stampede of wild horses than do anything that would hurt you."

His finger lightly ran along the curve of her waist and over her hip. "I am sailing into uncharted waters, my dear. You must assure me that you will not allow me to do anything that you are not comfortable with."

"I love you, John," she sighed as he trailed kisses along her jaw. Katie's stomach fluttered. She could scarcely breathe.

"And I have loved you since the day I first saw you on the riverbank," he replied with a smile. The hidden promise in his words created excitement, and scared the daylights out of her at the same time.

Katie sat in a rickety, weathered cane chair by the railing. "Before or after I almost drowned in that silly skirt?"

John slipped a matchbook under one of her chair legs to steady it. He sat in the chair facing hers. He pulled hers closer, until their knees bumped and their noses were only inches from each other. He creaked his chair back and forth a couple times.

"That silly skirt, as much as it could have done you in, turned out to be the best thing that ever happened to me." John's hand traveled along her thigh to her knee.

She tilted her head at that and smiled. "My knight in shining armor." She stared at the knot of his tie as he loosened it.

They slid slowly from their chairs to the wooden surface of the deck, still warm from the sun as their passion mounted.

He rested his hand behind her neck and gently pulled her down toward him until their lips were touching. His fingers crept upward to entwine themselves in her hair. He softly flipped her onto her back and hovered over her. Then as the night air seemed to become part of their embrace, everything else faded away.

As John began to remove the one article of clothing still in his path, he hesitated slightly. He swept the curve of her jaw with his lips and inhaled. He hoisted himself onto one elbow and looked down at her, his fingers brushing the hair away from her face. "I would hate to have my knight in shining armor badge revoked."

A heartbeat passed before she said, "Not by me."

Just before their lips touched again, he asked, "Are you certain of this, Katie?"

Katie nodded and the twinkle in her eyes dared him. She breathed softly in his ear.

"Aye, aye, Captain."

She rested her head against his chest, listening to the beating of his heart.

"Katie, my dear Katie …" He stroked her hair. "I don't want this night to end."

"We have tomorrow," she softly told him.

He inhaled deeply and exhaled before he said, "I'm afraid my brother has my evening planned for tomorrow." He frowned. "I can't think of anything I would rather do than spend the evening in your company."

Katie's eyes brightened. "But we can still see each other after I leave the market, before I go home, can't we?" She glanced at him, straining to see his reaction to the suggestion.

John rolled her over on her back and stared down in her eyes.

"Just try to keep me away, my dear."

She answered him with a smile.

John meandered back down the path leading from Katie's house to the road. He wandered and found himself back on the dock, studying the water and the sky.

He didn't know how long he stood there, but it was long enough for the light evening rain to flatten his hair and drip down the sides of his face.

The woman possessed a mystical window that somehow allowed John to see the world through different eyes. His smile spread to a wide grin as he strode down the pier and resisted the urge to shout.

However, it had created a dilemma for John as well; the plight was serious. Somehow he had lost his heart to a woman he'd only known for a few weeks, and he hadn't even properly courted her. He would have to do his best to correct that.

The rain had slackened to a fine mist as he approached the porch steps of Will's house. John stopped; He hadn't realized something until that moment.

He was whistling; he was actually whistling.

John walked carefully through the cramped parlor but, being darker than when he walked through the room during the daylight, he knocked over a small bookcase. Muttering to himself, he set it back upright and put the books back.

There was one still on the floor, splayed open, revealing an envelope. He leaned over and picked it up. As he tucked the envelope, securely, back inside the front cover, he instinctively opened it back up.

John studied the envelope. It was addressed to a Kathleen McGuire. *What an interesting coincidence.*

He wondered if there was any relation to Katie's Aunt Rose. He stopped. It was beginning to dawn on him that it might not be a coincidence. An aching cavity formed in his chest.

*What have I done? What have I gone and done?*

## ~ Fifteen ~

JOHN'S THOUGHTS CHURNED all night long. He rolled onto his side, then flipped to his other side – and then back again.

In the morning, he followed the sound of whistling, where he found Will in the barn, adding hay to the loft. John drew in a ragged breath as he looked up. "Morning, Will."

Will peered down over the rail at him, his angular face breaking into a wide beam. "Yes it most certainly is." He picked up a pail and turned away. "I'll be down in a minute."

* * *

Will looked over just as John sat on a stool by the stall.

John's heart banged in his chest. He sat back on the stool, unable to clear the scene with Katie, from the previous day, from his head. He had to tell Will he was hopelessly in love with Katie and he could not bear to give her up.

He studied his brother. He leaned toward him, elbows on his knees, as if he was about to close an important deal. He took a deep breath and began to form his words.

But before John could open his mouth, Will leaned in, clasping his hands between his knees, and spoke first. "John, I know you will say it's too soon, but I truly feel my chances dribbling away." He pulled in a breath and blew it out. "Not only do I plan to tell her my feelings, I am asking Kathleen …" He paused. "… her name is Kathleen … to be my girl."

John felt like a deflated balloon. An ache spread through his chest as he realized the prognosis. He conjured up the vision of their father, many years ago, his words resonating back and forth, bouncing around in his head:

*"In the end son, the only thing you will always have, through thick and thin, is family. It's the most important thing you will ever possess."*

John slumped, without a word. He blinked, though he wasn't blinking back tears. He felt heartbroken and furious in the same moment. He searched his brother's eyes and closed his mouth.

If this was God's plan, he would not interfere, no matter how much pain it would cause him. He closed his eyes and fought to conceal the rage and anguish that were tearing him apart.

William noticed John's uneasiness. He could feel the tension that settled through him. There was little doubt in his mind that turbulence was stirring. And it had something to do with Kathleen. "Are you alright, John? You don't look well."

Sweat beaded John's upper lip - a nerve twitched in his jaw, just before he spoke. "Actually, Will, I came to tell you I am leaving – going back to Cleveland tomorrow." The words tasted like dust.

*✲ ✲ ✲ ✲ ✲ ✲ ✲ ✲ ✲ ✲*

John suspected William hadn't believed a word he had said about why he was leaving to return home so abruptly; that he suddenly needed to oversee the repair of a freighter in his fleet. His presence hadn't ever been required in the past.

Will did find it odd, indeed, since the first time John mentioned that he might leave early, he had said it was to close a business deal. That was an obvious contradiction of stories.

John just hoped that his brother would never figure out the real reason.

"If Kathleen and I marry, our family will have a woman's touch once again." Will laughed and patted John on the back. "Just think about it," he said.

As if John would be able to think of anything else.

*⁎⁎⁎⁎⁎⁎⁎⁎⁎⁎⁎⁎⁎*

"You have nowhere else to be, John. I had hoped you would want to spend your last evening here with me, at the festival - especially since your visit has been so abruptly cut short."

His mouth went dry as Will spoke, and he began pacing around the barn, casting his eyes anywhere but at his brother.

John stumbled over the first words and paused to inhale one last breath of cool evening air before he began hinting to the events that had transpired over the last few weeks.

It only took a few minutes for Will to catch on. He glared at his brother. He leaned back against the railing to balance himself. He was stunned. Tense lines appeared on his face.

"Do you really think I would have…" John left the thought dangling.

Will's hard jawline was taut, his control fragile.

John went on. "Katie … Kathleen, had no notion that I was your brother, nor did she ever try to put ideas into my foolish head."

William couldn't look at him. He felt a huge sense of betrayal. He threw back his head and laughed.

John forced a smile, touched William on the shoulder, and he continued. "Will, please don't be angry with Kathleen."

However, as he started to leave the barn, the light from outside was suddenly cut in half as Will blocked the doorway. He wiped his face with the sleeve of his shirt and spoke. "At the moment, John, *you* are the one I am angry with."

The two men halted within inches of each other. Will pushed John backward. But when Will raised his arm to deliver the blow, John grabbed hold of his fist. His face contorted as he fought with his emotions. Anger, frustration, and a whole host of other emotions that he wasn't used to coursed through him.

They were nose to nose again. "I'm not fighting you, Will. You already won."

Will pulled his fist away from John's grip. He shot daggers of contempt at his brother. John quietly walked out the door without bothering to close it behind him.

# ~ Sixteen ~

THE LIGHT IN KATIE'S eyes was luminous as she approached him. She smiled; the look was unmistakable – she was in love. He stared at her for a long moment, the sparks of a still undeniable connection going off between them

But John approached her somberly.

At first, she didn't understand what he meant, and she thought he was joking, but she soon realized he was dead serious.

"Katie …" He saw the hope light in her eyes as she fidgeted, clasping and unclasping her hands, listening to his words. She stared at the ground.

Her hands immediately stilled, and when she finally looked up, he hated the shadows he saw in her eyes. Katie's eyes searched his face for answers he was somehow hiding from her. It was as if the man she had grown to love over the short span of two weeks, just ceased to exist.

Each time his eyes met hers, he wanted to hold her and tell her how he really felt, and take her away with him – as far away as he could from the rest of the world. And every time, his thoughts were interrupted by the image of Will. His smile had seared John's conscience.

Reality had set in; his expression hardened slightly; ice settled in John's stomach. His focus tightened.

"I will be on my way back to America in the morning."

Her mouth twisted in an uneasy smile. Her effort broke his heart. He could see how devastated she really was.

"I believe I understand, sir." Her trembling lips made another feeble attempt to smile, as she held her hand out and touched his sleeve, then quickly withdrew it. "May you have a safe trip back home. Goodbye Captain."

The red rims around her eyes exposed the true state of her mind.

He drew in a long, trembling breath through his nose, then kissed Katie; a kiss that was only meant to say goodbye. When her lips turned salty and wet, John realized he was tasting her tears. Gently, he broke the kiss. He couldn't bring himself to look at her.

"Goodbye Katie. Promise me you'll be careful swimming in the river." He fought the urge to run his fingers through her hair. He made himself look away.

*She's not yours.*

Katie fought the ridiculous desire to throw herself at him. Instead, she pulled away, straightened her shoulders and lifted her chin.

With guilty tears stinging his own eyes, and his face burning almost as much as his heart hurt, John turned and walked out of Katie's life.

He almost spun back around - the urge to go to her, to take her in his arms and beg for forgiveness was so strong he felt choked by it. He continued off at a brisk pace and she stared at his straight back as he walked away from her.

John's rejection hurt a lot more than Katie let on and by the time she arrived back home, it had evolved into a physical ache. How could she have misread John's signals so badly? What did she miss?

Katie wilted.

⁎⁎⁎⁎⁎⁎⁎⁎⁎⁎⁎

William spent the afternoon convincing himself that he was the winner in the contest, and whatever had happened between his brother and Kathleen would go away in due time.

The last thing she had been in the mood for was the Quinn's Harbor Festival that night, but she had promised a dance with a few of the loyal customers from the market; the event supported the town.

That evening, William escorted Kathleen home after the celebration. When they stopped at her front door, he leaned in to kiss her – their *first kiss*.

It was a nice kiss, but Kathleen's lips felt wrong; there were no flying sparks.

A victory. Why didn't it feel like one?

And in that moment he knew he had been kidding himself into believing that he could make her forget his brother.

William didn't go home that night. He didn't return until dawn. He was vaguely aware of the shadow waiting for him as he approached the steps, where he met John on the back porch. Neither said anything as they entered the house. The silence between them was louder than a shouting match.

John went to his room and closed the door behind him. He packed his bags, finding himself jamming his fist into the mattress several times, in frustration.

Will and John exchanged a few civil words; mostly about his voyage home and the weather. As the stable wagon pulled away, Will wiped his brow and returned to the house.

If he hadn't been so miserable, John would have paid more attention to enjoy the scenery along the route to the depot, with its freshly dewed color and vibrancy, but that just wasn't in the stars. His heart was heavy as he entered the train station. A dark look clouded his eyes, but he managed to conceal it with a weak smile.

Physically and emotionally exhausted, Captain Stockton drifted off to the lullaby of the train rumbling out of the station.

## ~ Seventeen ~

ROSE KNEW SOMETHING was wrong the moment Katie walked through the back door into the kitchen that morning. The sadness in her heart was more than obvious.

Katie knew lingering fantasies about *that* night with John would haunt her for the rest of her life. Heat washed up her face. Did he think of her as a shameless trollop? He said he needed her. Did he mean only in *that* way?

"Katie girl – What is it?" Rose called her into her little bedroom, behind the pantry. She sat on the edge of the bed and gently patted the spot beside her with her hand.

Katie had always loved and admired her Aunt Rose, a strong woman, quite progressive for her time, who lived her life with absolute passion. She would know what to do – she always had the right answer to the question. Aunt Rose was afraid of nothing, and Kathleen Rose was proud to have been named after her.

Rose had taken in 5 year-old Kathleen when her sister-in-law, Molly, passed away, at the age of 23. Rose's brother had left the family shortly after Katie was born and they never heard from him again. Sometimes at night, Katie could still feel the touch of her mother's hand as she reached over and laid it atop hers the morning she passed. The moment took her back in time.

*Her fingers were ice-cold; her face had lost all color. Molly must have seen the panic in Katie's eyes the moment her daughter grasped the significance of the moment.*

*"Katie ... please don't cry. Would you like to help me feel a little better?"*

*The five-year-old nodded with tears welling in her eyes.*

*Her breath was extremely shallow but her mother managed a smile and said, "Maybe you could tuck that blanket in tight around me to keep me warm – you know, like I did for you when you were just two years old."*

*Katie quickly reached around Molly and did so, tears streaming down her face. Then she climbed into the bed next to her mother and laid her head on her chest. She listened to the sound of the wind in the trees.*

*"Feel my love ... always, darlin'. And never be in such a hurry that you can't take the time to show kindness; to feel the sunlight on your face." Then, as she reached to stroke Katie's hair, she inhaled one final time and whispered, "Promise?"*

*Little Katie clung to her mother and cried. "I feel it, mama. I promise."*

*Then she was gone. Gone with the peaceful grace of a rose petal breaking away from a bloom, escaping in a gentle breeze.*


It was a painfully young age to endure such a loss. But with Rose's love and devotion, Katie never wanted for anything.

"Is Will calling after his brother is on his way?"

Katie stood. "Brother? Oh Rose, Will has no family; I already told you that."

Rose looked at her with surprise. "Of course he does. His brother John has been visiting for the past few weeks. All of Quinn's Harbor knows that. How is it that you haven't heard?"

Her face void of expression, Katie sat back down on the bed. She reached for her hanky and blew her nose. Then, as her eyes met her aunt's, the pieces of the puzzle began to make sense.

Katie poured out her heart and soul to her aunt – she unabashedly filled her in on everything that had happened over the past two weeks – all of it.

It took Rose a moment to untangle Katie's sentences. But once she realized what she was trying to tell her, she just let her spill it all out.

When Katie had run out of words and her tear supply was on empty, Rose wrapped her in a hug and then released her with a sigh. Then she stood. She smiled at Katie and put her hands on her hips. "Do what I have always done. Pride can kill your soul. Follow your heart. I have never regretted it."

## ~ Eighteen ~

KATIE HELD TIGHTLY to the horse's mane and gripped with her knees as they raced on against time. She took a shortcut through the woods; a branch smacked her in the face but she didn't flinch. Continuing east, she pressed the steed harder. A thick cloud of smoke caught her eye, as she reached the Quinn's Harbor station.

Katie barely had time to tie her horse before she ran into the station. She burst out the door of the depot out onto the platform and observed the tail end of the early morning train pulling away.

Thick, weathered hardwood planks clanked beneath her boots as she ran across and down the boardwalk. She rushed as fast as her legs would take her, the lace at her wrists fluttered like butterfly wings, crying out his name.

"John – John!"

Katie threw caution to the wind and leaped off the platform. In an impulsive move, she sprinted down the tracks. But she was too late. She would have been faster, but the heels on her boots slowed her down.

John was sound asleep, as were the other passengers on the early morning route; nobody on the train heard her, so it continued on its way. She began to lose hope, pitifully losing ground as the train gained momentum. About 500 feet down the track, she tripped, skidding to a halt.

Panting, she hopelessly gasped out the word a final time:
"John …" Her face blanched and her breath left her. She wheezed, then clutched her chest. A deep sadness welled up inside Katie.

With the expression of a woman whose life had just come to an end, Katie felt all hope slipping through her fingers, while she helplessly watched the caboose get smaller and smaller until it disappeared into the horizon.

## ~ *Nineteen* ~

*October, 1911*

EACH NIGHT, BEFORE he went to bed, John arranged his clothing for the following day. On the upholstered chair at the side of his bed, he laid out what he had selected to wear – not just the pieces, but each in his own, unchangeable, order as to how he would put them on.

A heavy rain fell his first night back home and as it pelted the roof, John tossed and turned, eventually finding sleep. He woke up exhausted in the morning.

He had a flying dream. In the dream, he was sailing with his father and his uncle along a rocky shore, chatting about nothing in particular, when a breeze picked up. As John held out his arms, he was lifted up into the sky by the wind. He rose higher and higher, over the water toward the stars – the world below him lost all detail. The sky was perfectly quiet.

For what seemed like hours, he was soaring, descending and sailing, floating through the clouds. As he looked down, he saw his father and uncle waving to him; his father speaking, but he could not make out what the words were. Then he noticed that Will was with them. John woke up. He yanked the covers over his head and fell back asleep.

He did everything he could think of to pull himself out of it, fishing, going on bike rides and flying kites at Edgewater Park, but it was all he could do to keep his head above water. His days followed the same routine.

Saturday morning, with a slight sense of anxiety, he went for a walk, and somehow found himself standing on the shore of Lake Erie.

Autumn had definitely arrived. It was amazing how different the weather was from only a few weeks earlier. Mornings were crisp and quite chilly while the days were warm.

The trees had exploded in shades of russets and orange, creating a riot of color. But as he watched the confetti-colored leaves sprinkle down on the sand and rocks, the only color John could see in his head was green - wild clover and emerald-green grass dancing across a meadow; a meadow in Ireland.

Spring, summer, autumn, winter – for the captain, the passing of the seasons didn't seem to matter anymore.

Silence enveloped the air around him, an emptiness haunted by the sounds of the water breaking against the rocky shore. He was trying to forget Katie ever existed, and failing miserably. The blush on her face … the sparkle in her eyes. Underneath it all, the memory of her face, her body, her fire, gnawed away at him.

The knowledge that this woman could still reach inside him made John want to scream.

Katie had branded John's heart forever.

~ *Twenty* ~

FOR THE FIRST DAY, they had remarkably managed to avoid the mention of Kathleen's name, or bringing up John's visit to Ireland at all.

Two weeks prior, he had sent William a wire, asking him to come to Cleveland. It was the first face-to-face meeting they'd had since John's return home. He thought it was important for them to clear the air – especially since Will would undoubtedly be bringing Kathleen into the family soon. And maybe he could convince him to join in the shipbuilding business with him.

Because of the splendid weather, the lake was busier than usual for mid-week. John was a passenger on the vessel's maiden voyage, a small passenger steamship that had been adapted to a ferry, along the Cleveland lakefront to Edgewater Park.

It was the latest of a number of smaller-scaled excursion steamers converted by Stockton's shipyard, and he had invited William to accompany him for a leisurely cruise around Cleveland Harbor.

On the right, the lake gleamed all the way to the Canadian shore. John pointed out a string of barges loaded with coal making their way toward the river.

"How often do the barges come through the harbor?" Will asked.

"Oh, every few days or so." John smiled, keeping his eyes fixed on the lake.

To John's chagrin, Phoebe Simpson had gotten wind of their trip and had secretly arranged to be aboard for the excursion. Her eyes sparkled, and she shot them a brilliant, empty smile. He rolled his eyes at Will as they watched her board with the other passengers. Seated at the front of the ferry, she positioned herself so that she could easily slip in next to the captain.

Phoebe, with her figure, buxom full but narrow at the waist, seemed to cast a spell over men. Her skin was nearly as white as the lace around her collar. Her motives however, were never as pure.

At the front of the bow, John stood for a moment and held the railing with his right hand; his left hand in his pocket. Somehow, Phoebe materialized next to him. He barely flicked a glance at her.

She wouldn't have complained if he had put an arm around her shoulder. In fact, she was actually considering how far she would let him go on a first date.

Phoebe's fingers closed over John's. Their hands together; the feeling carried her to a place she didn't want to leave. However, he quickly pulled back his hand. John turned away, without a word, joining the ferry captain at the wheel. He pulled out a clipboard and filled out a report.

John conversed with William, pointing out Cleveland lakefront landmarks as they plied along the Lake Erie shoreline. Off in the distance, a pair of box kites jousted with each other in the wind off the lake.

William divulged to John that he found the women in Cleveland very attractive; almost as beautiful as the women in Quinn's Harbor. John awkwardly said nothing. But as William continued with his story, he described a particular young woman in quite detail, and it didn't conjure up the image of Katie at all, in John's head.

John cornered Will. "Who in tarnation are you talking about?"

Upon further discussion, John realized that the young lass Will was referring to was not Katie at all.

Her name was Maggie. A measured smile inched its way across the captain's face. He was hit with a sudden, unexpected picture of what his life could be like. Up until that moment, John hadn't allowed himself to imagine or envision a life, of any kind, with Katie.

In the span of less than a minute, he went from zero to one thousand. Had he found just cause for merriment? A relieved laugh spilled out of his mouth.

The realization that he cared so deeply for Katie flooded him with elation, hope and misery, all at the same time. It converged upon him, like a landslide.

John cleared his throat to speak, but the words died on his lips, leaving his face void of expression.

Along the lakefront, just west of Edgewater Park, sat a stretch of vacant land. Inhabited only by trees overgrown with wild roses, it astounded him. As it passed them by, he was further drawn in by a massive old oak at the northeastern edge of the tract. Swaying in the summer breeze off the lake, it towered above the rest of the trees, as if it was personally motioning for John to set foot on the property. Like thousands of tiny winking stars in the sky, it beckoned to him as the sun caught gaps between the feathery leaves, allowing them to sparkle with an uncanny brilliance.

Imagination or not, John found it impossible to ignore. His hair stood on end as he visualized himself ... a house ... Katie ...

His grin flashed again.

All at once, John Stockton took the wheel from the ferry captain, and suddenly turned the boat around in a sharp gyration of a twirl.

*"Captain Stockton!"* The ferry captain shouted as passengers slid from their seats into a pile of derby hats and petticoats onto the floor of the vessel, Phoebe at the bottom of the pile.

While Will and the ferry captain scrambled to assist the horizontal passengers back to their original vertical places, John continued to stare at the shore. He fell in love with the smiling lip of land that looked out over the quiet twist of the shoreline.

The idea of a house on the lakefront brought light to John's face. He would build Katie's home on Lake Erie.

At Captain Stockton's request, the excursion ferry drew closer and John studied the shoreline; the land that lay just beyond its rocky cliffs, and he conjured up the image of a house.

Not just any house – *the* house. It would be grand. He knew what had to happen next. He must find the man who held the deed to the acreage that ran along the lake.

They hadn't had time to reflect; they had been so intent on the rescue effort. But when it was all over, and they were alone, Will and the ferry captain doubled over with laughter, recalling the expression on Phoebe's face as she attempted to straighten her hat while still in the prone position at the bottom of the pile. The ferry captain laughed so hard he had to grab Will's shoulder for support. But Captain Stockton didn't even know what had happened; he was oblivious to anything else.

The house would be fabricated with materials originating from the actual land it would be built upon; it became John Stockton's obsession from that day forward.

## ~ Twenty-One ~

KATIE BECAME WEAK and listless over the months following John Stockton's return home to Cleveland. She retreated from her own life, rarely spoke and she barely ate enough to stay alive. Spending most of her time in bed, her friends could not pull her out of her deep depression. It was a side of her that nobody would ever have guessed existed.

The month of September changed over to October. Katie's aunt opened the door to her room, stepped inside and quietly closed it behind her. "Katie – you have a visitor."

Red edges around her eyes exposed the true state of her mind. "I don't want to see anyone."

"Katie, darlin' please."

"Go away!" She pulled the blanket over her head.

Aunt Rose left the room with her head down.

Voices just outside the door spoke first in soft tones, but as the conversation went on, the hushes evolved into an argument so loud even Katie couldn't ignore it. Frightened, she strained her ears.

"You can't make her see you if she doesn't want to see you. Go now." Then it sounded a like a muffled squabble followed by a little scuffle. "There – I've locked the door! You'd best be on your way now."

It became surprisingly quiet on the other side of the door. Katie slowly slid out of the bed and, quiet as a mouse, tiptoed across the floorboards. She crept to the door and listened with every bit of attention she could muster up.

Suddenly the door to the bedroom was forcefully kicked in. She jumped backward, nearly losing her balance. William Stockton stormed into the room with Aunt Rose on his coat tails, her mouth hanging wide open. His brown eyes flashed in Katie's direction. He crossed the room in three strides and took hold of her arm.

The girl flew back into the bed and hastily threw the blanket over her head.

"You can't hide forever, Kathleen." Will's compelling voice carried across the room.

She refused to acknowledge him. He marched to her bedside and after a slight hesitation, he drew in a long breath and he continued.

"Well, since there's nobody here, I might as well sit down." And he seated himself on the big, blanket-covered lump on the bed. It squirmed.

"Ouch! You're hurting me! Go pester somebody else, please!"

Will said nothing. And he didn't move.

Aunt Rose's muscles tightened, but she refrained from taking any action.

From underneath the covers, the muffled, infuriated voice continued, "Are you trying to kill me?"

"I think you are doing a fine job of that by yourself." Will replied.

The lump wiggled out from beneath his weight. Katie sat up, pulled the blanket off her head and she found herself nose to nose with William.

"Why are you here? To make me feel worse than I already do?"

His boyish grin brought a sparkle to his eyes. "Ah, there it is. I knew there was something about my Maggie that reminded me of you – that must be why I was so suddenly smitten with her."

After a moment, Katie straightened up. Her face lit up like a firefly. She squeezed William's arm. *"Maggie?"* she asked with a degree of excitement in her voice.

Will gave a glance in Rose's direction.

Rose had always liked Will; there was something about him; a genuine kindness - it must have been in his upbringing. She saw the twinkle in his eye, and she nodded, slowly backing out of the room, to leave them alone. If there was anyone who could bring Katie around, she knew it would be him.

William had been concerned about Kathleen and things he'd heard about how her fiery zest for life was dwindling.

He finally asked her, "Mind if I ask why you are still in bed in the middle of the afternoon, Katie?" He winked, but he could see the sadness in her eyes.

She froze at the sound of Will's voice, calling her "Katie." He had never called her Katie before. The resemblance of Will's and John's voices was uncanny at that moment. It was almost as if John had just said it.

Suddenly she grabbed the blanket again, flipped over and turned her back to him, in silence.

It was Will's intention to call her by that name – he knew very well that, in the past, he had only referred to her as Kathleen. He was curious to see if that name would force something to snap. A mischievous smile tilted his lips. But now that it had happened, he wasn't exactly sure what he should do next, to bring back the Kathleen he used to know.

He looked at her with a smile and he let his instincts kick in.

Without warning, William ripped the blanket off her bed. Katie sat straight up. Her eyes widened with shock.

"Leave me alone!"

He didn't. Instead, he picked her up and carried her outside, to the trough used to water the horses, while the furious Katie screamed and kicked - even biting him one time. He stopped at the trough and held her above it. She looked down, then back at him. She puffed on the curl that had fallen out of her combs, tickling her nose.

*"Oh, you wouldn't dare!"*

"I wouldn't, would I?" And he released her.

She hit the water with a colossal splash, spooking the horses waiting patiently for their afternoon drink. As she rose from the water, she pushed her hair out of her eyes.

Half reclining, half-sitting, with water dripping down her face, Katie glared back at William, as he turned to walk away.

"You're not going to just leave me here like this, are you?" She was mortified.

Will pivoted on his heel and stepped back in front of Katie. He tapped his boot on the ground beneath him. He scolded her.

"If I had a lick of sense, I might."

Katie tried to get up but he wouldn't let her; he pushed her back.

"You'll get out when *I say* you are ready to get out. Now, sit down."

She sat on her backside, with a splash, blew out a frustrated exhale and eyed him indignantly.

William smiled at the sight of her, looking like a drowned rat as he watched her attempt to stand, only to slip and fall back into the trough again. She folded her arms across her chest and frowned up at him.

William's eyes twinkled as he went on. "I dare to say I am not certain why John is so fixed on taking on such an impetuous woman as his wife."

Katie's jaw dropped - her eyes widened. 'What did you say?"

William squatted down so he could look directly at her. Face-to-face, she could see the dark intensity of his eyes.

"I said I suspect that John intends to marry you." He reached in the pocket of his jacket and pulled out an envelope. "It's all in this letter. You may read it for yourself, once you've dried out."

She opened her mouth to argue and he shoved the envelope in it.

William winked at Katie as he helped her out of the trough. "That is, unless your answer will be "No."

## ~ Twenty-Two ~

ONE AFTERNOON, A FEW weeks later, a wagon pulled into Quinn's Harbor, stirring up a cloud of dust in front of Maguire's Market.

Katie was in the back, washing fruit, balancing baskets, when one tipped, sending apples rolling in all directions. She dropped to her knees and muttered,

"Get yer wee selves back here."

She crawled toward the main walkway, her backside in the air, gathering the rogue fruit into her skirt. She chased the final one just as it hit something. Katie turned her head slightly. She couldn't see anything but legs, but her eyes followed them upward and she froze.

She could never forget those storm-tossed-sea eyes. Her heart clutched. Was he real?

Captain John Stockton. He was studying her closely. The air whooshed from her lungs as she uttered his name. "John." She couldn't help but smile.

John held out his hands to her and he beamed. "Katie."

Tears appeared in her eyes as she forced a nod. She couldn't form any words, but she took his hands as he helped her to her feet.

John found himself nearly overwhelmed. He was silent for a moment, and then he went on.

"I don't suppose you could spare a few moments ..." he paused at a loss for the perfect way to say it, "for an old friend?"

She glanced over at the line of customers at the counter. "I've about an hour before I leave for home."

The familiar Irish lilt made John's heart skip a beat.

"May I return and see you then?"

Katie nodded, momentarily dazed, but as the line of customers grew in length, she glanced back at them.

"I will see you in a short while, my dear." John said quietly, with a reassuring smile.

*He said,* ***my dear****!*

When John returned, he had left Will's wagon at the house, choosing instead to walk the mile back to the market. As McGuire's came into his sightline, his eyes searched, but Katie was nowhere to be found.

He stood in front of the market sign, expressionless, with his hands on his hips. Then, just as he turned to look in the other direction, he sensed her at the far end of the stand.

Katie stood in the afternoon sunshine, smiling at him. She had just finished hitching the horse to her cart.

He helped her get up onto the wagon. She picked up the reins. John didn't bother to walk around the wagon. He climbed up and slid as close to her as he could, taking the reins from her. John released the brake and gave a flick of the reins. "Go, now." And the horse started walking.

She struggled to determine how much she could really say and how much she should keep a secret. About a mile out of town, John tugged at the reins, and the horse obediently halted. He set the brake.

John took Katie's hand and held her gaze. "I've lived with this shadow over me for months." He ran his finger under her chin.

"I know this is anything but proper, but I don't know any other way to say it." He rubbed his thumb over the back of her hand. Those dark lashes of his swept up and down.

His heart gave an uncomfortable thump at the sheer thought of Katie being an ocean away. His eyes boring into her soul, he said, "Marry me, Katie."

Katie's eyes widened. Will had given her the idea that this might happen, but she wasn't sure exactly how he would do it.

Her eyes turned soft and liquid.

"May I tell you something?" He touched her cheek. "I had a difficult time after I went back to Cleveland." He had a pensive moment. "When I was happy ... and also when I was sad, I thought of you."

She looked at him carefully. "Why?"

"Because you saw past the facade; the man everyone thought I was. And somehow you still cared for me."

Katie smiled. "Yes, John, I will marry you."

## ~ Twenty-Three ~

JOHN AWOKE TO FIND birds chirping outside his window. He bounced out of bed early. This was the day. He knew it would take him longer to groom himself today; every hair must be in place. He grabbed the razor and stopped to smile at the mirror on his way to fill the water basin.

But before he reached the door, there was a knock. He opened it to find Will standing there, holding a delicate hanky, slightly yellowed with age, embroidered along the edges with tiny pink flowers.

"Yes?" John said, his angular face breaking into a smile. Then he noticed the hanky Will was holding out to him. "Will, is that mother's?"

Will nodded. "This is something I have had in my dresser since she died." He unfolded it and refolded it, looking down.

John said, quietly, "She would have adored Katie, you know. I wish she could have been here for this day."

Will smiled. "Maybe there's a way we can make it possible."

John gave him a puzzled look, but Will grinned from ear to ear. "Never you mind. I will take care of everything." And he walked out of the bedroom, with John falling into step behind him.

Katie had gone through her entire wardrobe at least a dozen times, trying to settle on what to wear for the ceremony. She narrowed it down to an ivory-colored crepe dress with a pink sash at the dropped waist and a creamy yellow two-piece frock. She decided on the ivory garment.

Aunt Rose beamed when her little girl entered the bedroom and stood before her. She moved Katie back into place so she could do up the pink shell buttons on the dress.

There was a soft knock at the door. Rose cracked the door open slightly while Katie arranged her combs, intently studying herself in the mirror.

"Kathleen, you look like a princess," the voice spoke gently from behind her reflection. She leaned slightly to one side, revealing William Stockton, grinning at her. Katie shifted from one foot to the other, then turned to face him.

Her eyes filled, but he held up his hand. "No tears. This is the happiest day of your life, as it is for my brother as well. "He smiled and stuck his other hand in his coat pocket. "I have something I think would make our mother very happy, if you would be so kind as to carry it on your wedding day." Will pulled out the hanky that had belonged to their mother.

Katie held it to her cheek. "Oh, it's lovely."

He touched her hand. "The story is that our mother carried this on the day she and our father were married, back in Chicago."

"Of course I will carry it with me." She turned to Rose, who helped her tuck the hanky in the pink sash at the front of the dress.

Rose stood back, next to Will and sighed. "It looks as though it belongs there, doesn't it?"

Will nodded. "Perhaps it was meant to be."

Rose patted William's arm and nudged him toward the door. "Now then, Will, you'd best be tending to the groom. See to it that he gets to the courtyard on time." She winked. "I wouldn't want him to change his mind, now."

Will laughed as he closed the door behind him. "I'm not the slightest bit worried."

They had made the decision early on to have a small, quiet outdoor wedding in the marketplace courtyard, but somehow everybody knew everything, right down to the last detail, and the electricity flowing through Quinn's Harbor for the days leading up to the occasion was unmistakable. In the end, the entire town was in attendance for the wedding of Captain and Mrs. John Stockton.

Katie's hair was swept up slightly, with tiny pink and white rosebuds pinned at the crown, secured with combs that matched her auburn tresses. She looked like an angel floating on air, with Rose walking down the garden path alongside her.

John Stockton tried to keep a straight face, but his joy was difficult to hide when he caught his first glimpse of his bride. John's eyes sparkled with unshed tears when he saw the delicate little hanky, tucked into the sash of her dress.

After the ceremony, the mayor of Quinn's Harbor tinkered with his box camera, insisting on so many photographs of the happy couple that they were beginning to wonder if they would ever find the time to be alone.

Rose finally pried him away by inviting him to join her at O'Brien's. Before long, the celebrations had commenced.

Although the captain and Katie had long disappeared from sight following the third party, the celebrations that followed lasted well into the wee hours of the next morning, spilling out into every pub along Belclare Street. And at every establishment, Will was tasked with yet another toast to the bride and groom, which he was more than happy to oblige to.

"So, where, might I ask, will the newlyweds be taking up residence?" Michael inquired as Will landed on a stool, wedged in between Jimmy and Brady McCarthy at O'Brien's.

"John is building a new house. The final verdict is not in yet, but he wants to bring her home to Cleveland when it is finished."

You could have heard a pin drop.

"Will - that can't be!" Jimmy turned to him. *"Say it isn't so."*

Will tipped back his mug, then he set it on the bar in front of him. "I'm afraid so. My brother is a bit of a perfectionist. And he refuses to bring Katie to America until her house has been completed."

Michael leaned in. "Knowing Katie as well as we do, I imagine she's not taking to the news very well, is she?"

Will broke into a smile the way other people broke into a song and dance. "I believe her words were ..." He stood and good-naturedly did his best impression of a woman. "I would rather live in a *chicken coop* than to be without him."

They all laughed, but they knew she meant business.

The McCarthy boys raised their glasses. And the few who were still coherent enough to join them did the same.

*"To Katie and Stohn Jockton!"*

The newlyweds took the wagon back across town and onto the road to return to the cottage John had rented for the week. The days that followed passed in a blur.

In a battle of wills, even though she was the more stubborn of them, John won out in the end. Katie would remain in Ireland until the house was complete.

John pulled his eyes away from Katie and surveyed the train. He whispered in her ear then tucked her arm through his as they walked on the platform to the waiting passenger car. Katie glowed, thrilling at the word "husband" when she heard people referring to them. She tiptoed up to kiss his cheek.

He stood, waving, from the open car door as the train lunged slowly forward. Katie leaned around a pillar and cupped her mouth with her hands. "I love you!"

Rose walked back to the wagon with her arm around Katie's shoulders.

## ~ Twenty-Four ~

JOHN MET THE CONSTRUCTION supervisor at the building site for the new house.

"Sure is a pretty piece of land, captain," he said as he unrolled the blueprints on a crate. He turned to face Lake Erie and added, "There is no better stretch of real estate in the whole city. I still don't see how you convinced that old spinster to sell – she swore she'd *never* let go of it." He laughed. "We thought we would be planting her here someday."

John chuckled as he recalled the first of a dozen meetings he'd had with Miss Eva Cleary.

Eva Cleary, a former schoolteacher from Virginia City, Nevada, who fancied herself as a writer-of-sorts, had become reclusive and unapproachable in recent years.

Eva had relocated to Cleveland, to care for her aging father, who had been given six months to live. As sad as that was, the timing could not have been more perfect. Miss Cleary had been a victim of malicious local gossip, resulting in the loss of her teaching position, and the situation provided a convenient reason for her sudden departure in 1886.

It was actually a rather intriguing story; a scandalous love affair with a well-known American author, and although she vehemently denied it and nothing was ever proven, the fascination and the gossip refused to die down.

She never proved it didn't happen either; she didn't think she needed to.

Rumor had it that Eva Cleary had been seen in the man's company in New York City, on more than one occasion. Naturally, there was nothing to substantiate any inkling of inappropriateness, but the story seemed to take on a life of its own.

To Eva, he was much older and wiser than her, a mentor; someone she'd admired and looked up to. He had given her advice on writing and warned her about the unsavory world she might encounter as a female author in a man's world.

Miss Cleary had been getting along fairly well, following her father's death in 1887. Choosing to remain in Cleveland, she kept herself busy writing tales. Only known to her, she had stashed dozens of unread manuscripts in hidden, secret drawers of her father's desk.

In 1910, at the news of the death of her mentor, she ceased writing; the desire and drive just died with him.

Miss Cleary was annoyed at the audacity of the captain, suggesting that she sell her prized lakefront property. Her lips were pressed so tightly together that they almost disappeared into her face.

She told him to go away.

He did. However, he returned two days later, with flowers. The third time John arrived with flowers and something else – his journal.

On that and each visit that followed, he allowed her to read an entry from his journal; the story about the love of his life, Katie – how they met; how he pursued her. And how they almost lost each other – in great detail.

By the sixth visit, she actually appeared to be looking forward to the latest chapter in their saga; her eyes lit up like stars at the sight of the captain's journal. On his twelfth visit, Miss Cleary opened her front door and greeted him with a genuine smile as he presented her, once again, with flowers; a bouquet of fragrant roses. This time, she invited him into the parlor for tea, which gave him renewed hope. John opened the journal to the next entry about Katie and handed it to her.

Eva took her time reading the entry while the captain poured himself a cup of tea. And he watched her face – for what he wasn't sure. Her lips moved soundlessly as she followed the words on the page. She looked up from the book. "And you never gave up on her?"

"Ma'am - with all my heart and soul, I knew she was the only one for me."

Eva stood and handed the journal back to John. "Thank you, captain. I have thoroughly enjoyed your writing. You have a gift for making the reader dream that she is the one you are writing about."

John stood as she handed it over to him. He started to speak, but she quickly interrupted him. "There is however, one flaw in your most recent entry."

John, head still, glanced at her with his eyes.

She pulled back and gave him a schoolteacher's stern look. "It's dreadfully incomplete."

Confused, he watched the old woman reach under the parlor table. Miss Cleary pulled out a large envelope and she opened it. The paper rattled as it unfolded.

"Ma'am?" the captain asked.

"A good writer must see a story all of the way through." She smiled through twinkling eyes. "You have another entry to make, captain."

He tilted his head to one side.

She handed John a pen and went on. "Can you take dictation, Captain Stockton?" She pushed the inkwell toward him.

He didn't know if he should say yes or no, so he said nothing.

She rapped him on the knuckles, with the rolled-up paper, as if he was an unruly student who wasn't following directions. "November 2, 1911." She peered over his shoulder to see if he was writing.

He was afraid not to, so he started at the top of a new page. Then he hesitated, waiting for additional instructions.

She dictated further. "Today I signed the agreement, allowing me to purchase the land along Lake Erie, in the area known as Edgewater, in Cleveland Ohio, from Miss Eva Cleary."

John dropped the pen, but Eva didn't hesitate. In a stern voice, she said, "Captain, I must see your entry before I can give you a proper grade." With a shaky hand, John wrote the words in his journal.

Nobody else understood what really turned her. But he knew.

Within two weeks, the property belonged to John Stockton and construction had begun.

John scrutinized the quarry stone foundation and inspected the logs slated to be on their way to the mill the following day.

"We'll put the framing up in the next week."

"And with any luck, the new market project will be complete by the time we need the interior carpenters."

John nodded in agreement. He knew very well that an undertaking as large as the market on 25th Street would take precedence over a single house, no matter how important the owner was.

## ~ Twenty-Five ~

LIGHT-HEADED AND GIDDY with excitement, Katie clutched the paper to her chest and looked up into the sky.

It was a one-way excursion ticket to New York City, in America. As she read on, her excitement mounted.

Arrangements would be made to transport her to Southampton, where she would be among the first passengers on the maiden voyage of a new luxury steamship, the RMS Titanic. From there, she would travel by rail to Cleveland, Ohio - to her future.

She wondered how she would ever be able to wait – April 14 was five months away.

* * *

John frowned as he drove up to the building site. When Timothy, the foreman, had telephoned him to meet him there, he had neglected to tell him that one of the trees he had chosen to save, a beautiful oak, had been the victim of a storm the night before.

Lightning had struck the old oak tree, splitting it in several sections. The branches of the split, fallen tree seemed to move as if they were alive as John stepped over them. His frown deepened.

"It's a shame, isn't it?" Tim said as he approached John.

John nodded, his gaze fixed on the trunk and the ground beside it.

Tim put his hat back on and said, "Lightning hit it, right down to the roots. It never stood a chance." He bent over to brush off the knees of his pants. "It's a stroke of luck that it didn't fall the other way – it could have caused some serious structural damage."

John swore under his breath. He stooped down and sadly touched the fallen tree. It had been the one that he'd had big plans for – the only one on the lot that had a heavy branch at just the right height for a swing. There was something so special about that majestic tree; he'd been drawn to it the first time he'd set foot on the lot.

John turned to walk away, but something caught the edge of his vision. He kneeled down at a large section of the trunk where the bark had been partially burned off. He studied it close up. He stood and walked around to the opposite side. Then he backed up and stared.

No matter what angle he viewed it from, it still looked like it. John's heart flip-flopped.

A combination of the natural movement of the grain, the remaining slivers of bark and oddly placed scorch marks from the lightning strike had left something behind - the faint outline of a compass rose. John looked over at Tim, who was peering at him curiously. "Don't you see it?"

Tim shook his head and scratched his cheek, dismissing John's question. John, feeling the doubt that appeared on Tim's face, spun back around and his face fell. He didn't see it anymore either. It was gone.

*What an imagination I've acquired.*

Tim reached down and snapped off a thin twig from a dry branch and threw it. "Don't worry, John. We'll get a crew in here this afternoon and dispose of it."

"Say Timmy!" John stood. "You don't suppose it could be salvaged, do you?"

Tim looked at him as if he had lost his mind. "For what? We already have everything we need from the trees we sent to the mill."

"How about the front door?"

"What?"

"You know - the front entrance door of the house."

## ~ Twenty-Six ~

*March, 1912*

KATIE'S FACE FELL. It was a telegram from John Stockton. In it, he explained that the completion of the house had been temporarily delayed, due to a combination of weather complications and a major city construction project in Cleveland, called the West Side Market, which had taken precedence and was creating a shortage of skilled labor.

John Stockton absolutely refused to bring his bride to America until her home was complete – that was it – simple and final.

Katie fought a downward tug on her lips when she broke the news to her aunt. She arranged a pyramid of apples on the market table and declared, "Oh, I cannot imagine how a simple fruit and vegetable stand could set back the completion of our house, but if that's what John wants, I won't make a fuss over it."

That turned out to be a bit of a mixed blessing. It didn't take long for the news to begin trickling into the shipyard. The activity on the Cleveland waterfront was buzzing.

The door to John's office flew open. "John! The Titanic sank!"

"What?" John scrambled across the office to observe the pulse of panic out on the docks. "That's impossible! It's only her first time out." He grabbed his jacket and ran out into the street. One of the shipyard welders was wandering in front of the building, slightly dazed, when John stopped him.

The man stared back at him, in horror and grabbed John's sleeve. "She hit an iceberg ... thousands of people are dead!"

Horses clip-clopped down the street while the sporadic motorcar beeped for right-of-way. John pushed through the gathering, curious crowd and hurried to the telegraph office next door. He rattled the locked door handle incessantly, until he got the attention of Matthew Wilhelm, the operator. He looked up, recognized Captain Stockton through the glass and, after a slight hesitation, came to the door and let John inside. He locked it behind him and inhaled deeply.

John approached the telegraph and watched in shock as the news continued to stream in.

Wilhelm tapped a pack of cigarettes, pulled one out and slid it up to his lips. He struck a match then offered the pack to John.

John hesitated for only a moment, and then he took it, realizing that it would be his first one since the day Lucas Camden passed.

With a shaky hand, John swooped the cigarette close to his mouth, held it there and struck a match, touching the flame to the tip. He inhaled deeply and forced out a narrow draft of smoke.

Matthew looked over his shoulder at John, the visor hiding his expression. "This is fresh off the wires, John; let's not get carried away, just yet. You know there are bound to be inaccuracies."

"You're right. Maybe it's not as bad as it seems." Nevertheless, John had a terrible feeling about this one.

It wasn't until much later, when John grabbed a newspaper, dated Tuesday, April 16, 1912, from the top of a stack, that it began to sink in.

It couldn't be. He had to read the headline four times before his brain processed the words:

TITANIC, WHITE STAR LINER
SINKS ON MAIDEN VOYAGE AFTER COLLISION
WITH ICEBERG APRIL 14 - 1800 FEARED LOST

## ~ Twenty-Seven ~

"WILL, COME IN." He heard Rose say from the stove.

He opened the kitchen door and stepped in. "I don't suppose you've heard."

"Heard what?" Rose stirred the stew and moved the pot aside to allow it to cool. She wiped her hands on her muslin apron. "Don't be telling me you've brought bad news."

The sound of the coil on the screen door interrupted them, followed by Katie. When she saw the look on Will's face, she blanched. "What is it, Will?"

He removed his hat and sat at the table. "The Titanic went down."

Katie and Rose stared, in silence.

"She hit an iceberg. Last count I heard, there were more than fifteen hundred dead."

"Oh dear - all of those poor people ..." Bewildered, Katie clutched at her chest and sank into a chair. "I could have been there; I almost feel as though I *was* there, with them – so much pain ... such grief."

Rose reached up high, and opened the tea cupboard over the stove. "Well I, for one, would like to thank the good Lord that you weren't." She stood high on her toes, reaching as deep as she could, to the back of the cabinet. She rummaged around, blindly until she snagged a bottle, catching it just as it dropped off the edge.

Will's eyes twinkled. Katie's widened. He quickly stood and took the bottle from Rose. He turned it so he could read the label. "Why, Rose, Where did you ever find this?"

Katie stood. "What is it?"

"The best …" He cleared his throat. "… *Paddy* Irish whiskey." He laughed. Katie sat back in the chair with a thud.

Rose blushed as Will handed the bottle back to her. She set it on the table, and retrieved three small clear glasses. As she placed the glasses on the table in front of them, she sighed. "I have been known to need something to keep me calm – to quench my thirst on occasion." She uncapped the bottle. "And this evening, with that bit of news, I find myself *particularly thirsty*." She pulled out a chair and sat.

"Aunt Rose!" Katie raised her voice in a loud whisper. She fingered her collarbone.

Will smiled as he quietly poured the Paddy Irish in each of the glasses, then he lifted his to the ladies at the table.

## ~ Twenty-Eight ~

*May, 1912*

"AUNT ROSE – WILL STOPPED by the market this morning - says he'll be stopping by this evening." Katie opened the screen door and placed a basket of apples on the kitchen floor.

"He'll be stayin' for supper then?" Rose asked.

Katie laughed. "I told him you would give him no choice in the matter."

Rose met Will out by the barn with a basket of pears as he hitched the horse and wagon to the post. "Before you have the chance to forget."

He took the basket from her and winked. "You are a true angel, Rosie. If I were just a bit older, your heart wouldn't be safe."

She laughed. "Young man, I'm afraid I'd be more than you could handle."

He reached inside his jacket as they walked to the house. "I heard from John yesterday."

She raised her brows. "Any news about the house?"

Will tucked her hand in the crook of his elbow and they stepped up on the porch.

After supper, Will wiped his mouth with a napkin and pushed his chair back. "Supper was as tasty as ever, Rose."

Katie couldn't contain her excitement and curiosity any longer. She leaned in. "So what news have you brought me, Will?"

"The house is getting close to being finished."

Her eyes lit up. "Will I be joining John soon?"

Will reached into his jacket. "There are tickets already reserved for the two of you at the Quinn's Harbor train station. Rose will accompany you to Queenstown."

"When?" Katie asked him.

"June. Actually, the tenth of June." He handed the brochure to Katie, but Rose grabbed it and began reading it aloud.

"The RMS Laconia … to Boston."

Katie chimed in. "Where's Boston?"

Will laughed. "Boston is a city in Massachusetts. It's not as big as New York, but it's larger than Cleveland." He turned the pages of the brochure and let them study the pictures and the itinerary John had written on the back.

"John has arranged for the two of you to dine at one of the finest establishments in the city. You will spend the night at the Commodore Hotel. Rose will accompany you to the port, where she will see you safely onto the Laconia."

"After your departure, John has made provisions for Rose's return to Quinn's Harbor."

## ~ Twenty-Nine ~

KATIE HAD ONLY BEEN on a train once before in her life. It was shortly after her mother's death and she had been joining Aunt Rose on the journey to what would become her new home – Quinn's Harbor.

As she finished packing her suitcase, she drifted off into the recollection.

*Five-year-old Kathleen squirmed in the agonizingly upright wooden pew-like excuse for a seat. It was cramped and torturous and smelly. As she had walked down the aisle to her seat, she felt the stares of the other passengers, evaluating her. She hated it.*

Katie sighed, snapping the suitcase clasp on her finger. "Ow!" She sucked her finger and sat on the bed again. "Oh, Aunt Rose, what if I cannot be everything that John wants in a wife?"

"Nonsense." Aunt Rose reached out and patted her arm. Rose latched her case for her. "Now, shall we go? We don't want to be late."

***

It thundered and loomed past the platform; the train rattled and screeched to a halt.

As Katie and Rose approached the platform to the first-class compartment, a uniformed man took Katie's hand to assist her in climbing the steps. Perplexed because her skirt, which she had just received from a friend of John's, in Cleveland, was so tight, she stopped and stared back at Rose.

Rose giggled at her dilemma and told her, "Child, that's what God gave you a brain for."

Katie didn't give it another thought; with her spare hand, she hitched it up and stepped onto the first rung.

The seats in first-class were upholstered and tufted in maroon velvet. Katie found her seat and sat back, closing her eyes.

The train suddenly lurched forward and gradually settled again as it let out a hard whistle. Katie opened her eyes and turned to the window. The world she had known for fourteen years was slipping past her.

A lavish suite, overlooking the harbor, with peacock wallpaper, ivory drapes and bedclothes appeared in front of them as the door opened.

Katie and Rose spent the evening in Queenstown. After a dinner fit for royalty, they returned by taxi to their suite. Katie seemed a little melancholy to Rose - something she felt a need to dispel as soon as possible.

With Katie's hands in hers, she said, "Katie girl – this is my dream come true … that you have found your one true love. And that you are happy." Rose smiled. "John will give you a wonderful life."

"But Rose, I will be lonely without Quinn's Harbor; without you."

"Och - I will be but a few days away. I will visit you and you will visit me. Why, you might be so happy that you will forget me altogether." She winked at Katie.

Katie's eyes filled. "Please don't make jokes about this."

Rose patted Katie on the back and headed to the bathroom. She returned amid the sound of running water. "I think you will feel much better after you've had a nice hot bath."

Katie emptied a bottle of lavender milk into the hottest water she could stand. She stepped in and soaked for an hour as the stress of the trip and any anxiety leading up to it floated up and out in the steam through the transom.

## ~ *Thirty* ~

AS LUCK WOULD have it, the New York Central with Katie onboard made its approach to Cleveland during the tail end of a mid-June storm. The rain had ended but the robust wind gusted as the train continued along, running parallel with the lake.

The engine rocked; the passenger cars shimmied. The woman on the other side of the compartment held herself still as if the least bit of movement would upset the train. Katie hung onto the armrests of her seat. She wanted to close her eyes, but the excitement and curiosity gnawing at her soul would not allow it.

The man traveling with the woman continued chattering away, keeping Katie engaged in conversation. She listened with half an ear while she enjoyed watching the scenery pass. So many houses; each of them was home to someone.

Katie leaned against the window, hypnotized by the blur of stone structures and brick warehouses that lined the landscape. Black steam poured out of smokestacks from the factories off in the distance. Each vision brought her closer to a life very different from what she knew.

She was intrigued by steamships filled with cargo and tugboats coming into view on the horizon. She wondered if any of them were part of the Stockton fleet?

The train came to a slow, hissing stop at the station.

The air smelled of metal, brine and oil. The conductor helped Katie down the steps to the platform.

She stood on the platform among her trunks and hatbox. The granite pillars towered over her as she searched the faces of the men, several with stares lingering on her, for the gentleman who John said would be meeting her to bring her home. She picked up her hatbox and looked up and down the tracks.

Katie was beginning to become worried that she had misunderstood her instructions, when a voice from behind her calmly said,

"Mrs. Stockton."

She jumped. If the voice had been any closer, it could have bitten her.

The man leaned back against the bench, driving cap pulled down lazily over his eyes. He crossed his leg and smiled in her direction. She turned to face him. He removed the hat and held it to his chest.

Katie's eyes widened as he stood.

She flew into his waiting arms. The air whooshed from her lungs as she cried out his name, "John!"

He tightened his arms around her, capturing her close to his heart. Time stopped as they stood on the platform in a tight embrace, neither of them able to say anything.

A giggling toddler broke their trance. He kissed Katie gently, then gave her a look that made her go weak at the knees. He lowered his forehead to hers and rested for a moment.

John picked up her hatbox and escorted Katie into the building. "Your trunks will be in the vehicle by the time we get out there."

She tilted her head slightly. *A vehicle; not a wagon?*

Voices inside the building echoed off the high ceiling and marble floors. Polished wood benches were filled with people, waiting for their trains, bags at their feet.

John let go of Katie's elbow and stopped in front of a motorcar. He ran his hand proudly over the engine's cover and smiled. "She's a 1911 – a real beauty, isn't she?" John made sure the tool kit on the side of the body was locked. Then he opened the door for Katie.

She climbed into the passenger seat. John turned the choke lever, then cranked the engine before stepping up on the running board. "I love this Packard, but I'll be glad when I have the new one with an electric starter."

John's fingers curled around the steering wheel as he slid into the driver's seat. The engine came to life. The roar echoed through Katie's head, and with every rumble, her excitement climbed. He eased the auto into first gear.

Spark plugs firing, the car whisked them along their way. A runaway lock of hair swept across his forehead as he pushed up the brim of his cap. He brushed it away but it escaped again, resting just above his dusky eyes. Katie let her lungs take in as much air as they would hold before breathing out again.

The light turned red and John hit the brakes. Katie studied her surroundings, trying to memorize every little detail, her eyes eventually settling on a set of pillars that curved, joining themselves at the top.

A scrolled ironwork sign set into the arch read *EDGEWATER*.

At the green light, He pushed the gear lever into first, and proceeded forward. They motored down a brick lane, the lake running the entire length of the street on the right. He eased off on the clutch and let the gas out a little.

At a stop sign, John pushed the bill of his hat a bit higher, revealing a gaze of excitement. Gas flowing without restraint, the car surged forward and Katie's heart soared.

"Almost there!" he shouted, his voice sounding farther away than it actually was.

She saw a big house about half way down the curve in the street. Trees blocked some of it from view, but even from the distance and with the towering oaks, she could see it stood at least two stories high and had several steep sloping roofs that reached into the sky.

John steered the car into the circular drive and stopped in front of a two-story carriage house sporting a charming little window facing the lake, very similar to Katie's window back in Quinn's Harbor, except it had a railed Juliet balcony.

Katie loved the protective ceiling of Spruce and Hemlock; the way they shaded the yard and the drive leading up to the house. She found the scent refreshing and clean.

There it sat – their home, beautifully framed by azure blue skies and puffy white clouds, flanked by vibrant blooms of the wild rose gardens.

Handbag swinging from her wrist, Katie passed the sundial as she sauntered through the rose garden on her way to the front entry door. Young blooms of pink and scarlet, sprinkled with tiny apricot yellow buds drew her nose to their honeyed fragrance. Enclosed by a hedge lay a cobblestone path leading to the front of the house.

John unlocked the door and it opened. Katie was speechless. The wood floor in the foyer shone, dancing with the reflection of the brass chandelier and its tiny glowing electric candles. She turned to John and whispered, "I love it!"

Katie dropped her bag as John scooped her up to carry her across the threshold. She giggled when he stumbled a bit, but he quickly regained control. On the other side of the door, he gently set Katie back down and grinned. "Mrs. Stockton – Welcome Home."

The house's interior reflected a combination of tastes: the captain's, which was classic, and Katie's, which radiated warmth and comfort. Katie was amazed to see many of the personal treasures she had grown up with while living with her aunt.

She crossed the foyer to the table at the base of the stairway and picked up a tiny black enameled box, decorated with a delicate pattern. It had belonged to her mother, and Aunt Rose kept it in a bookcase next to her bed.

His eyes refused to waver from hers as he watched her tears well. He opened the box, still in her hand. "I had it made into a music box for you." He leaned forward to listen. She smiled back at him.

John took the box from Katie and placed it on the table. He took her hand in his; they fit together well as he escorted her to set of massive, double pocket doors. He released her hand to part the doors, and revealed another room.

A grand, sun-washed room, filled with windows.

He traced the line of her cheek with one finger as he watched her eyes. "Are you happy, my dear?"

"Oh yes, very," she said, smiling, as their lips met.

Just when Katie thought John had finished the tour, and she had begun up the staircase to open her trunks, John jumped in front of her on the steps. "Not just yet." He smiled and placed her hand in the crook of his elbow, steering her back down to the main floor.

She looked at him with a curious little smile.

"There's one more thing I must show you." He grinned as he escorted Katie out through the kitchen door to the front of the carriage house. He unlocked the door and led her to a flight of steps at the back of the building. Once they had reached the landing at the top of the staircase, John stood back and allowed Katie to explore on her own.

She ran her hand along the walls, clad in birch paneling, as smooth as a baby's behind. She stopped in front of the window.

"I wanted a bigger window there; it looks out over the lake. But the pitch of the roof wouldn't permit it." John told her.

"It looks like my little room, back in Quinn's Harbor." She walked across to the window and looked out. "How perfect."

John beamed from ear to ear, with pride. He wrapped his arms around her shoulders from behind. "You can count the lights out on the lake at night, just like stars." He held her face in his hands, his gaze serious. "I want you to feel at home in this space."

She walked curiously to the door next to the chimney. "What's in here?"

A wry smile tugged at his mouth. "Actually, that's a design flaw. He laughed. I was so intent on providing a room for you to use as a retreat, that I didn't notice an area of wasted space in the plans until it was too late."

"What a beautiful door. It looks like a piece of art."

"It's special. I had it milled from the same oak tree that the front door was crafted from."

"Is that where all the doors came from, John?"

John shook his head and answered, "No … it was so bad we could only salvage enough of the tree for the two doors …"

She saw the look of disappointment in his eyes. "What a shame, John."

He broke the moment of silence. "… and the new ship's wheel for the *Compass Rose.*" He smiled at the thought.

She grasped the door handle. It didn't budge. "What's in here?"

"It's just storage, for now." He covered her hand with his and rattled it.

Something was wrong with the doorknob. He took a key from his pocket. It didn't insert into the lock properly. He pulled harder, forcing it and a bolt fell out of the knob. Screws and pins scattered across the floor.

"Well I'll be damned." John followed, with an apologetic glance, for his language. "Sorry." He rubbed his chin.

He fumbled a little and jammed the pieces of the knob back together with the hope it would stay in place long enough to get the door open.

John tried to turn the doorknob. The door resisted. It stuck for a moment, then yielded. He yanked with all his might, and it flew open. Nippy Spring air flooded the attic as John stepped into the room. The moment Katie turned to return to the window, a swift breeze kicked the door shut.

John pushed on the door from the inside with no luck. Evidently, he was trapped.

Katie heard the pounding on the door from across the attic and returned, easily opening the door, revealing her grinning husband. "I'll get the carpenter back here first thing in the morning."

## ~ Thirty-One ~

THE NIGHT AIR WHISPERED through the open windows as a light rain danced on the rooftop. John worked on his journal while Katie finished the mending.

He was in the middle of a thought when there was a knock at the door, disturbing the tranquility of the evening. Katie put down her mending, but John quickly jumped up first and headed to the foyer.

"I'll answer it."

He opened the oversized, solid oak door. A generously proportioned woman with flame-red hair pulled back tightly in a bun, swept into the foyer, the tails of a fox-fur boa, riding in her wake.

It was no secret in Cleveland that Mrs. Simpson had long set her sights on Captain Stockton as a suitor for her niece, Phoebe, who had just returned from a trip abroad.

"I had every intention of being here much sooner, Captain Stockton, to meet your bride and discuss your July reception details, but I saw the most divine stole in the window at Higbees, and … well …" she dramatically rearranged the boa, switching shoulders as she tossed the tails.

"… I just couldn't resist."

John smiled and reached out to help her remove her wrap, but she slipped through his fingers and waltzed across the foyer to the living room.

Katie stood and felt the woman's critical eye on her from the doorway. Mrs. Simpson's lips twitched, but she managed a smile. Her ruby ring, flanked by diamonds, flashed in the moonlight filtering in through the picture window as she approached.

John caught up with her as she entered the room. "Katie – this is Mrs. Abigail Simpson. Abigail – my wife, Katie." Katie offered her hand and Abigail barely brushed it.

After a few moments of idle chit-chat, mostly about Abigail's life, Katie jumped in. "Where are my manners? Mrs. Simpson, allow me to make us some tea." She left John at the mercy of Mrs. Simpson.

Fortunately for John, there was a knock at the door. He excused himself and left Abigail alone in the parlor. "Abigail, won't you have a seat? – Katie will return with your tea momentarily."

Mrs. Simpson spotted the journal, laying on the table across the room. Curiosity got the better of her; she decided she'd like to see what he was writing. She made sure she wasn't being watched, and took a few sidesteps. The captain's journal seemed to taunt her, daring her to pick it up.

Abigail Simpson was never one to spend much time weighing the pros and cons of her potential actions, so she swept the log off the table and opened it.

Giving a muffled snort, she thumbed through the log until she hit something that caught her attention. She read on, eyes widening with surprise, the book slipping from her hands, when she reached the beginning of the entry where John first met Katie.

With a flick of her wrist, Mrs. Simpson grabbed the captain's journal and fanned herself.

She became so engrossed in his entries that she didn't see John at the doorway to the room. The moment her peripheral sent her the message that he was approaching, she quickly dropped it in the chair the captain had been sitting in.

"I apologize, Abigail – I didn't mean to be rude, but I had a small business matter that I had to address." John paused, as he got closer to her.

The journal was sitting on his chair when he returned to the parlor. Had he carelessly left it there? It was not something that he would have done. Then, from the corner of his eye, he saw a look of guilt appear on Mrs. Simpson's face as she glanced at the chair.

With no expression, he chose his next words carefully. "I have a way with words, wouldn't you agree, Mrs. Simpson?"

"Why, I don't know what you mean," she said, noting the growing intensity in his eyes.

"Did you manage to read it all, or do you need more time?"

She startled at the question and was unable to hide her surprise. "Whatever do you mean, captain?"

He laughed. "You were reading my journal."

She let out a breath and tried to hide her embarrassment. "The book fell to the floor. I was only returning it to the chair for you."

John's eyes narrowed with suspicion. He moved a step closer to her. Not knowing what else to say, Mrs. Simpson remained quiet. A silence hung between them.

Katie returned with tea. The air was heavy with unspoken words. She glanced at John – he gave her a wink.

Abigail took a few polite sips of tea before returning the cup and saucer to the tray. "I must be on my way. Phoebe will worry if I am late arriving home." She practically ran to the door, Katie following close behind her.

As Mrs. Simpson reached out for the doorknob, Katie smiled. "I do hope you will visit again soon, Mrs. Simpson. It was a pleasure meeting you."

Mrs. Simpson never turned around and continued hastily on her way.

Katie giggled and shook her finger at John when she re-joined him in the living room. "What did you say to that poor woman? She looked as though she'd seen a ghost."

He just shook his head and smiled.

*That poor woman?* Katie had no idea, but he knew she would soon find out for herself.

"Did you love Phoebe?" Katie asked John softly, when he leaned over to turn out the bedroom lamp that night. He looked surprised that she would ask such a thing.

"I saw the way she looked at you yesterday, when we were downtown." Her eyes met his over the fading light. She wished she could retract the question the instant it fell from her lips.

Katie's first impression of Phoebe was that she was looking at a French bisque doll. But that would soon change.

Even in the faint light of the moon, John sensed there was more behind her questioning gaze. He quickly turned the lamp back on, restoring the light in the bedroom and turned away, mumbling something under his breath.

Katie felt a flash of jealousy. She wanted to slap herself.

*Jealousy is a dreadful thing.* She felt jealousy consumed your positive energy, just so it could stay alive. It altered how you viewed things and complicated everything.

She knew John had a life before he met her, but her feelings were hurt that he didn't think he could be honest and just talk to her about the situation. "I'm sorry. It isn't any of my business."

John picked up his journal, and then tossed it onto the table.

"Phoebe," he said with humor in his voice, "only cares about one person – and that's Phoebe." He moved to the window and began to disclose the story.

"Mrs. Simpson used to be Abigail Camden …"

"Camden? Is she related to …?"

"Lucas Camden? Yes, she is his daughter. His wife died in childbirth, leaving Abigail to be raised by several nannies."

"Oh, that's so sad. Now I feel guilty for some of my thoughts toward her."

"Abigail led a quiet, rather sterile life."

Katie frowned.

"Until she met Arthur Simpson."

Katie smiled weakly.

"Arthur was … eccentric." John hesitated. "Abigail never forgave Arthur for choosing his own father's business, overseas, over her father's shipyard. But she was actually the one who originally told him that it was the only path that would provide the financial means to support their high lifestyle."

Katie tilted her head to one side, hanging onto his every word.

"They had no children; neither of them had an interest in altering their prominent existence to accommodate children. They were the toast of every town they visited, earning quite an infamous reputation."

"Abigail reveled in high society living. And although they remained married for a year after the money ran out, she spent those months living abroad, while Arthur chose to return to America."

Katie joined him at the window and sighed an exhale of empathetic melancholy. John placed both hands in his pockets. "But Arthur's brother had a daughter."

"He did?" Katie smiled with a cockiness that let John know she had connected the dots.

*Of course! Arthur's brother and his wife's daughter is Phoebe.*

John saw the twinkle in Katie's eyes. He smiled and faced her, taking her hands in his. "Katie – I am about to tell you something that is not discussed ... *ever* ..." Then in a voice just over a whisper, he said, "Phoebe is actually Abigail's daughter."

Katie dropped to the bed with a thump. Her eyes widened. "No!"

He nodded and faced her. "Abigail always resented the fact that her extravagant lifestyle had to be curtailed when they ran out of money, and she divorced Arthur."

Katie sensed that the story was about to get very interesting. Crossing her arms over her knees, she sighed and her eyebrows shot up.

John went on. "Abigail, almost immediately, set her sights on Arthur's younger brother, Gerald."

"But I thought you said the family money was gone."

"Only Arthur's money. Gerald was very conservative, and hadn't taken on a wife." He frowned.

Katie remained silent but her responding smile was perfect.

"Phoebe was conceived while Abigail was still married to Arthur," he said quietly.

"Was that why she didn't come back to America?"

"I can't be entirely sure," he said. "But when she returned to Cleveland, she brought a little girl with her; a niece, about 6 months old."

"Phoebe. But why didn't Gerald provide for his daughter?"

"He did. He took care of Phoebe as long as he was alive and he left her a comfortable amount of money in a trust – funds that she squandered away within a few years."

"What about Abigail? Did Gerald marry her?"

"She had no interest in marrying again. Everyone still believes that Phoebe is Gerald's illegitimate daughter from an affair with a different woman."

"Oh."

"Gerald kept Abigail in her preferred lifestyle; he followed her around like a little puppy - God knows why; she treated him like he had the plague."

"Then, about two years before Gerald died, he met a wonderful woman; he wanted to marry her. But Abigail threatened to ruin him – and tell everyone that Phoebe was hers, if he married Francis."

"That's blackmail."

With another faint smile, he added, "Abigail believes that she is the rightful heir to her father's business. And she has tried every trick in the book to claim it for her own."

"Did Mr. Camden know about any of this?"

"Yes, he knew it all. Abigail was not very nice to her father when she began to suspect that I would be running the business after his death. She even attempted to have him committed, claiming that he was daft."

"That's horrible!"

"In the beginning, he set money aside for Abigail, but in the end, there was only a small fund, for Phoebe, in the will."

"Oh my. I feel bad for her."

"Don't. Somehow - God only knows how, she fell into another financial fortune."

Katie flashed John a smile. "Nevertheless, I shall never repeat a word of this. The secret is safe with me."

## Thirty-Two

HAT IN PLACE, LIGHTWEIGHT overcoat, sensible shoes and the only pair of silk stockings she possessed, Katie felt ready; she was confident enough to take on downtown Cleveland.

Abigail Simpson had dropped in early that morning, insisting on accompanying Katie to help her select a "suitable" frock to introduce her to Captain Stockton's society. Not at all happy at the thought, Katie had declined, telling Mrs. Simpson that she had decided not to go shopping that day; a white lie, because she couldn't bear the idea of spending any more time with the pushy woman than was absolutely necessary.

Her eyes widened as she watched the buildings and the people pass by the window of the cab. She leaned forward. "Stop."

The driver slammed on the brakes and glanced back at her with a puzzled expression. "Here?"

Katie reached in her bag and handed him the fare. "Yes, here. It's such a beautiful day – a beautiful city; I would like to walk to Higbees, if I may." She smiled.

The driver ran around to open the door for his passenger. As he pulled away, Katie stopped a woman, dressed in business attire.

"Excuse me, but how do I get to Higbee's department store?"

The hurried woman seemed surprised, but she did stop for a moment. She pointed her finger. "See that street up there?"

Katie's hand tented her eyes. "Yes, I see it."

"Turn to the right. Higbee's will be on your left …" then with a grin, she continued, "… after about 5 blocks."

Thirty minutes later, slightly out of breath, Katie stood on the opposite pavement and watched as customers pushed their way through the revolving doors.

She had never seen anything quite like them.

Katie approached, hesitating for a moment. Then, after watching five customers before her, she jumped into the first empty wedge that presented itself to her. She pushed through the divided pie, all but running to keep from getting her skirt caught in the turnstile.

She thrust a little too hard and found herself propelled into the lobby of the store more quickly than she'd anticipated. Katie gasped.

*Goodness, what a curious way to invite customers into your store.*

Higbee's department store had been around for years and carried a variety of things, from pianos to taffeta evening gowns.

The store was bustling with activity. A woman behind the glove counter looked at Katie oddly, as she regained her equilibrium, straightening her cockeyed hat. She realized how wet-behind-the-ears she must have appeared to the salesclerk, but she really hadn't seen a department store like that before.

Katie asked the woman, "I am looking for the ladies dress department." The clerk motioned for an older man to assist her.

He led her to an elevator with a metal mesh screen for a door and a uniformed gentleman with gold epaulets greeted her with a nod. "Good afternoon, ma'am."

When she hesitated, the first man gently nudged her across the threshold of the elevator.

Katie stepped deeper into the box and the man pushed the number '2' on a panel of shiny brass buttons after manually sliding the door shut. The elevator quivered to life with an aching jolt and began its ascent with slow, stiff jerks.

The elevator ground to a stop on the second floor. Katie stepped out onto marble tiles leading to a quiet alcove; a carpeted area lined with comfortable loungers. Elegance like she had never seen before.

Two sales clerks, each holding a hanger displaying a dress, immediately greeted her.

Katie searched for only 30 minutes before finding a dress she felt was perfect.

"How will you be paying for your purchase today, ma'am?"

Katie paused, hesitating for a moment with the realization that she hadn't actually said the words out loud before. "This will be charged to my husband's account."

The woman waited, pencil in hand for the rest of the sentence.

"John Stockton."

She gasped. Katie blushed at the woman's reaction. The sales clerk's firm lips softened into a smile as she scribbled on her notepad. She nodded. "Very good, Mrs. Stockton. Will you have this delivered to your address?"

Katie glanced at her fingers, clasped around the hanger, as if she wondered if it would disappear the moment she relinquished it. She shook her head. "No, I will take it with me."

Thrilled, holding her first official purchase as *Mrs. John Stockton*, Katie contentedly embraced the dress as she waited for the return of the elevator.

However, as the box began to appear, with the preview of its passengers through the metal grates, she felt her sense of contentedness dissipate. A sick feeling spread through Katie as she watched the woman get out of the elevator. She suppressed a frown. Mrs. Simpson had an arrogance about her that set Katie's nerves on edge.

*Trapped like a rat, with no way to escape.*

Abigail's hefty bosoms could have easily toppled her if she hadn't been so broad across the beam, providing a counterbalancing effect. She spoke with the measured tones of upper-crust Cleveland.

"Kathleen! Fancy seeing you here today. I had a feeling that you might have changed your mind. I just wouldn't be able to forgive myself if I hadn't tried to catch up with you."

*Wonderful. Simply wonderful.*

"Now Kathleen, let's have a look at what you have selected – I'm sure it's not too late to choose something more appropriate."

Katie drew her lower lip between her teeth and blew out a sigh of frustration. Why did she feel so awkward around the woman?

She had no choice other than to hold the dress up, slowly turning the hanger so she could view it from all possible angles. She glowed and fished for a compliment. "What do you think of this one, Mrs. Simpson?"

Abigail's nostrils flared as if she smelled a dead fish that had washed onto the Edgewater shore in a mid-August heat. "Well …"

Abigail began her critique, "This shade will look horrendous with your skin tone, and …"

Tears, hot and angry, began to fill Katie's eyes, but she successfully fought them off.

Mrs. Simpson went on. "Just look at the cut; it's outdated - obviously last years' design." When she couldn't pry the hanger from Katie's fingers, she sighed. "I suppose we could make do with it. After all – maybe everyone will understand … being that you are not one of us …" Then she quickly shifted gears. "But I am so glad I got here before you purchased your bathing costume."

"Bathing costume? Whatever would I need one for?" Katie asked.

"Don't tell me you have forgotten the summer picnic at Edgewater Park?" Abigail stepped backward, aghast.

Katie grimaced. She had forgotten about the picnic. And unfortunately, she did need a bathing costume. She didn't have any choice except to return to the women's clothing department. With Abigail Simpson.

They passed the combs, bracelets and necklaces displayed on the counters, along the way. Just past the millinery department, where she temporarily lost Abigail, Katie paused in front of a mannequin dressed in a dark blue bathing suit. She touched the collar, made of a silkier fabric, much thinner than the others on display were. She smiled as she followed the lines of the piping along the hemline.

"Ma'am, may I try this one on?" The salesclerk pulled out a hanger with a similar suit and handed it to Katie with a smile. It was a little shapelier than the first one. "This would be a better fit for someone as slender as yourself, ma'am." Katie loved it. She took the hanger and walked toward the dressing room.

Abigail resurfaced and flagged down the sales woman, just outside the fitting room. "Oh girl – show me at least a half-dozen bathing costumes … from the Nantucket collection; nothing too showy."

Mrs. Simpson disappeared with the sales lady, leaving Katie alone in the room with her thoughts. She made a face.

*But what if I* **want** *"showy?"*

Katie pouted. She looked at the suit she had brought into the room with her. With no hesitation, she began shedding her clothing. Once she was confident enough that she had everything secured in the proper places, Katie turned to face herself.

She stuck out her chest and buttocks and studied her reflection as she walked back and forth in front of the three-way mirror. Her posture was perfect.

Or so she thought.

The gasp could be heard throughout the entire second floor as Mrs. Simpson entered Katie's dressing room.

"Oh," said Abigail, flattening her hand over her heart. "This will *never* do! Take this away immediately!" She flicked her wrist as she exited the room, gesturing for the sales clerk to assist Katie out of the monstrosity as quickly as humanly possible. The woman made a secret face at Mrs. Simpson, causing Katie to giggle; something she quickly stifled.

Abigail scolded her from outside the dressing room door. "There are simply some things you may not wear - completely unacceptable for the *captain's* wife. And after you've found a proper costume, we will address the matter of how a true lady carries herself."

✶✶✶✶ ✶✶✶✶✶✶ ✶✶✶

"Are you ready, Kathleen?"

Katie shot her own reflection a frown. She did not like the suit at all. "As ready as I will ever be."

Abigail clasped her hands with delight. "Perfect." Katie winced.

Mrs. Simpson was quick to point out the flawed manner in which Katie walked.

*I suppose you are about to show me how it's done.*

Katie's face lost most of its color as she watched as Abigail, somehow managing to suck her belly in long enough to promenade around the fitting room, demonstrated to her how a lady must present herself in such attire.

"A woman's walk should be a work of art; beautiful and enviable – essential if you are to be a proper lady." She turned Katie to face her and demonstrated as the words fell from her mouth. "Back straight, chin up, ears in line with shoulders."

"Katie reluctantly obliged. "Shoulders in line with hips." When she wasn't satisfied, Mrs. Simpson leaned closer, grabbed Katie roughly by the shoulders, bringing a devastatingly pungent whiff of perfume with her. "Like this …"

Katie looked skeptical.

"Now, rise up on the ball of one foot, knee bent slightly, take long, sweeping strides."

Katie rolled her eyes but she tried it. She turned her ankle and caught herself by grabbing the curtain of the fitting room. The salesgirl caught Katie's eye with a wink as she backed out of the dressing room, leaning in with a final empathetic smile and a wave. "Have fun."

Highly unlikely.

# ~ Thirty-Three ~

*July, 1912*

CAPTAIN STOCKTON'S BARITONE echoed in the front hallway as he greeted his guests. The grandfather clock in the foyer chimed half past the hour.

Looking out the bedroom window, Katie couldn't take her eyes off the chauffer-driven automobiles that were dropping off guests to the reception. Her heart raced.

She took one last look at herself in the mirror and inhaled a deep breath, as she approached the top of the staircase. Nervous and anxious, Katie stopped just above the top step, unable to move her legs.

John had been conversing with city officials, recounting a humorous situation he'd found himself in on the previous day. The words sent them into peals of laughter as he shook his head.

The foyer became suddenly quiet as all attention turned, focusing on the landing at the top of the stairs. John pivoted on one heel as his eyes followed the staircase upward.

Katie was a vision in blue silk and cream lace. Her hair was simply atop her head with loose curls. He quickly ascended the steps to escort Katie to the party.

Captain Stockton couldn't help himself as he approached his wife. He felt the breath catch in his throat. "You look beautiful."

She was suddenly acutely aware again, of how attractive he was. And she was reminded of why she had fallen in love with the captain the first time she saw him. Katie smoothed down the folds of her skirt with her hands. "I feel out of place," she whispered to John.

"He leaned into her with a grin. "There's not a woman here who doesn't wish she could be you."

"Only because they want to be on your arm, captain."

The swell of the crowd quickly crested into happy applause.

She was a hit. Everybody loved Katie; her genuine smile, her natural beauty; all of them enraptured by her effervescence.

"Captain, Katie is simply lovely – I dare say it's a good thing she is already taken, for a line of gentleman callers would be at your door this very night."

John laughed and responded, "I am the luckiest man on earth."

From across the room, Abigail Simpson's eyes narrowed with skepticism. She leaned closer to her niece, Phoebe, her voice low and conspiratorial and hid her annoyance behind a fake smile.

Although she was truly enjoying the evening, Katie was still trying to adjust to being the center of attention – that was the part she was not completely comfortable with. Everywhere she tried to escape to, she found herself in another sea of bodies wanting to talk to her.

Nearly an hour later, the captain searched the crowd and spotted Katie, sandwiched in between Mrs. Simpson and Phoebe. He noticed an odd raise of the eyebrows, in a show of mischievous camaraderie, between the two.

Being stuck in the middle between the two of them had to have been uncomfortable, to say the least. John gestured emphatically in their direction as he made a beeline over to them.

Phoebe, with her outrageously curved figure clad in green taffeta, tilted her head back in the way she did when she felt threatened and wanted to show her superiority. She fluttered her eyelashes at him and touched his shoulder as he walked past.

But when John joined them, he placed his fingers over Katie's, and lowered his head to press a kiss upon her hand.

## ~ Thirty-Four ~

IT DIDN'T TAKE LONG for Phoebe and her girlfriends to slip out of their skirts and shirtwaists and into their navy blue bathing costumes. Square necked with tucked bodices and flared skirts, only varied by the details of the yellow or white piping along the edges; they showed more flesh than those donned by most other young women.

Katie fingered the hemline of her suit, and then sighed in frustration as she attempted to tie the kerchief around her hair, securing the bow in the front. Her eyebrows sank toward her nose.

They met, face-to-face, as they came out of the stall of the bathhouse. Phoebe adjusted her flowered swimming cap with a grin, and then disappeared with her girlfriends, down the steep wooden stairway like a horde of scurrying mice, and situated themselves on prime real estate – in front of the lifeguard tower.

Katie didn't have a flash about her like Phoebe did. It was more like a glow. She sat on the opposite side of the warm beach, digging her fingers into the deep layers of wet sand. She observed as Abigail sat down on a blanket so fast she miscalculated where the ground was, rear-ending it rather ungracefully. She giggled to herself.

Phoebe struck a pose for the lifeguard, then she caught Katie's eye; just long enough to let her know how she felt, then looked away.

John had carefully skirted any discussion of physical intimacy between the two of them, but Katie still wondered. She tuned them out and let her gaze wander over to the beach while she waited for John.

He took a few steps down the beach, watching the swimmers dive in and out of the lake. He sneaked up behind Katie and startled her. "So sorry I took so long. I had to take my girlfriend home first."

Katie took her kerchief off her head and playfully hit him with it.

"I had to make a stop at the market." He laced his hands behind his head and slouched lazily in a chair beside her.

Every time she looked up, John was staring at her. Studying her.

Just as lunchtime hit, Edgewater beach and the beach house became a flurry of activity, buzzing with loud merriment. John remained silent, with his hand on a basket, practically begging her to ask.

She caught his glance and giggled. "What's that?"

"It's our picnic lunch. I had Miss Pettigrew, from the market, prepare it for us."

Katie looked at him with humor in her eyes. "That's good John because, as you know, *we are* at a picnic."

"I know a better place for a picnic lunch."

Her ears perked up. She turned her head. "Where?"

John stood and held out his hand. He continued. "We have our very own little beach. It's beautiful – I want you to grow to love it as much as I do."

After they had changed back into their street clothing, John led her back to a tiny stretch of beach at the foot of the steps in front of their home – just beneath twenty-eight slabs of stone, each inching closer to the secluded beach off Edgewater, and the lake that lay beyond. And they set up their picnic.

John explained the lure of the lake and the sea. He found it difficult to explain why, but he was drawn to the water – and the mystery of what lies beneath its surface.

"It does frighten me though." Katie said, cautiously.

"You weren't afraid when you were crossing the ocean on your way home to me in America, were you?"

"Have you forgotten that I very well could have been a passenger on an ocean liner that met its fate on a collision course with an iceberg?"

John closed his eyes. "I most certainly have not. And I have thanked God many times for delaying the completion of our home, preventing you from being aboard the Titanic." He kissed Katie's hand. "But you arrived safely on another ship, didn't you?"

"I suppose you are right, but …"

"And aren't you the one who dared to swim in a raging river?"

"That was different, silly."

"I'm afraid I don't follow your logic."

Katie stifled a giggle. "I prefer to swim in shallow bodies of water. When I am swimming, I am in control. If I am not in control, I have no idea where I will end up." She sat next to John on the warm sand and ran her hands as deep as they would go. "Nothing good can come from the bottom of the sea."

"Some of the most beautiful pearls in the world reside in the depths of the water."

"Are there pearls in the lake too?" She reached down in her pocket and held out her hand. In her palm lay several tiny pieces of glass; beautiful fragments of long lost bottles, frosted and tumbled smooth by the time, sand and water of Lake Erie. She met his eyes with a broad grin. "Aren't these simply beautiful?"

John didn't think it was possible to love Katie any more than he already did, but as he studied the sparkle in her eyes, her appreciation for even the simplest of things, he knew he'd been wrong. He tried to keep his expression serious.

She saw through it and giggled. "You're laughing at me."

He took the glass chips into his hand and caught her eye. John feigned amazement. "My dear, I have never seen *lake pearls* more exquisite than these."

John took her face in his hands and planted a gentle kiss on her forehead. He held the "pearls" up to the light, then he asked her, "May I keep some of these?"

Katie nodded. "I can find more."

John grinned. "I think it's time you and I went on a boat ride."

She tensed.

"I will be with you the whole time, sweetheart. You will have nothing to be afraid of. The sooner you do this, the sooner you will see how unfounded your fears are.

She felt light as a feather. Walking on the deck, Katie stretched out her arms and legs, wondering if the lake breeze would pass right through her. The lake sparkled as if it was lit from below. Approaching him at the wheel, she watched the water form a V as the vessel cut into the lake, pointing the way.

John clasped his hands around her waist from behind as she relaxed into him, allowing the lake breeze to envelop her. He whispered in her ear as he felt her go limp. "See? There's absolutely no reason to be afraid, now, is there?"

She inhaled with a smile - a peaceful smile. She could get used to this life. "You're right John – I feel wonderful."

"Good," John said, grin deepening. "Because we're running out of gas."

Katie gasped, her eyes widening. She locked her knees to keep them from buckling. "Oh John – what are we going to do?" Her heart sped up.

The captain's stormy eyes narrowed in intense concentration. He said nothing. She couldn't understand how John could remain so calm in the face of such bad news.

He saw the fear growing in her eyes as she started to dart across the deck in panic. He caught her around her waist and reeled her in, gently grabbing her hand. He brushed the stray strands out of her eyes and he saw that she was terrified.

She looked back at him through blurry eyes. Her lips moved against his fingers as he shushed her, and she said nothing.

John tried for a mysterious smile. Then he calmly said, "My dear, ships have been traveling around the earth for centuries … long before fuel existed." He walked to the vertical posts and began unfurling one large and two smaller sails.

Shouting so she could hear him over the wind, he said, "It will take a little longer, but we will arrive at the same destination by this evening." Then he climbed the mast with a laugh and added, "I hope you don't have any other plans for today – because if you do, I think you will be late. You'll be stuck with me for awhile. Is that alright with you?"

"I can't think of anybody else I'd rather be stuck with."

From that day on, Katie began to take a far greater interest in John's fascination with the Great Lakes and the sea. She loved listening to his stories about distant parts of the world. He enjoyed teaching her as much as he could.

## ~ Thirty-Five ~

WHEN THEY ARRIVED back home, there was a delivery waiting for them on the back porch.

A desk. He recognized it immediately.

Solid Mahogany, it had cubbies on both sides and a large drawer in the middle. Sections that pulled out for writing convenience had hand-carved edges that matched the legs.

There was a letter attached.

Eva Cleary had left it to John in her will. These words, in her handwriting, prefaced the legal documentation:

*Tomorrow is the first page of your new story. Write a good one.*

*★ ★ ★ ★ ★ ★ ★ ★ ★ ★ ★*

The following afternoon, John spent hours polishing the desk after having it moved to his library. He was touched by the gift and the sentiment behind it.

After he positioned the banker's lamp, he opened the top right-hand drawer and removed his journal. He dated a new page at the top and began the entry telling about the day with Katie and the wonderful gift from Miss Cleary.

He finished the entry and yawned. John closed the journal and started to put it back in the drawer when he spotted something odd about the front of the desk.

His fingers traced engravings in the old, dark wood. On the face of each drawer, amidst an elaborately carved fleur-de-lis, there was a small, rounded-off square panel. Inside the panel of one drawer were tiny oval indentations. When he tried to open the drawer, it became apparent that it was not a drawer at all. Almost in a daze, John lifted his hand and placed his thumb, forefinger and middle finger into the indents and instinctively turned his wrist clockwise.

With no effort at all, the panel turned with his hand. After a quarter turn to the right he heard a click. It sounded like it was coming from the drawer he had open. He placed his hand inside the open drawer and gave the panel another slow, quarter turn. The back of the open drawer moved.

John jumped up, dropped to his knees, and met the open drawer at eye level. As he pushed the back of the drawer to see how far it would go, it fell off and disappeared completely down an empty space behind it.

He hastily pulled the remaining drawers out of the desk and studied the shell. He ran his hand along the front of the desk, rapping on it with his knuckles. He stopped. One place sounded different from the rest.

He found the nails that held the face board in place and carefully pried the board loose – just enough to be able to make out a stack of paper, laying at the bottom of a hidden partition.

A secret compartment! He smiled at the thought. Even though he knew the old woman wouldn't have placed anything of value in there, John was very intrigued by the notion.

He pulled out the last of the tacks and freed the desk panel.

John reached inside and first removed a small army – a fistful of lead toy soldiers, followed by a few papers, which had taken a severe, unyielding curl, held together by tacks. He studied the first page, then the second. He dropped the document and hurriedly retrieved the rest through the slot. The papers fluttered, faintly yellow-edged white in the sun drenched room.

They were manuscripts; stories that hadn't seen the light of day in decades. All written by Eva Cleary. John beamed as if he'd discovered a hidden treasure, surprised by the sudden sense of excitement he felt.

*＊＊＊＊＊＊＊＊＊＊＊*

The first stars were just beginning to emerge that evening, as John unlocked the door to the carriage house. He set the box of papers at the bottom of the attic stairway and took a quick step backwards.

He couldn't resist; he grabbed a soft rag from the table and dusted off the deep blue Packard. The new 1912 model, it had been in its new home for days, but he still felt the same as he did when he pulled it into the garage for the first time.

"John, did you take the papers? I don't see the box anywhere." Katie said, appearing in the doorway.

His mind snapped back to the task at hand and he retrieved the box. "I want to flatten the pages. There are some extra bricks up in the attic closet that I think I can use." He started up the stairs. "And if I leave the box in the attic, it will be out of the way."

"Good idea."

## ~ Thirty-Six ~

THE MARKET SAT ON West 25th Street, just beyond the intersection of Lorain Avenue, like a castle with its clock tower.

Eyes frantically bouncing back and forth between the clock and the long line of customers, the young woman searched anxiously. There was barely an hour left before closing time, but the cheese shop was overflowing with customers and clearly understaffed; short-handed.

A rather large man appeared from out of thin air, deliberately positioning himself directly in front of the display case with his hands on his hips. Obviously annoyed, he tapped his foot as his brows formed a 'V" over his nose.

A scowl creased Joseph Kelly's forehead. "Where is that French fool, Jacques?" he demanded.

Katie turned her head to listen.

"Just look at the business I am losing! I never should have taken pity on you and that worthless husband of yours! I should fire the both of you!"

"But sir, this is the first time Jacques has ever been late," she pleaded with the man.

Katie gave the young woman a sympathetic glance. Then she quietly slipped behind the counter, while the man continued berating the young woman for her inefficiency. Once he realized that her husband was not even present, he was absolutely livid.

Katie unpinned her hat and tossed it on a pile of boxes. Then she slid an unbleached muslin apron from a hook and tied it around herself, twice, securing a knot on her left hip.

Mr. Kelly saw her sneak behind the counter and he confronted her. "What do you think you are doing?"

"I am filling in for the man who is running a bit late."

"What?" He glared over at Adele. "Did you arrange this?"

Adele was frozen. But Katie stepped closer to the man and smiled. "Yes, she did - and I am very happy to be here, sir."

He was furious. He met Adele, nose-to-nose. "This woman knows nothing! You should be paying me for the lost business you have caused me. You and that useless husband of yours!"

Katie catapulted into the conversation. "Excuse me, but I believe I have a bit more knowledge than you might think, sir."

Kelly didn't believe her. He rolled his eyes, skeptically. "Oh, you do, do you?" He reached into the glass case and began carelessly carving tiny chunks from each wedge. "We'll just see about that."

The woman sent Katie a pleading glance to let it go – things were bad enough as it was. There was no point in digging a deeper hole than she already had. The last thing she needed was for the man to prove she was a liar and fire her. And her husband. They desperately needed their jobs.

Jacques and Adele Laurent had recently arrived in Cleveland from Paris. Although both were talented artists in their own right, neither had managed to find their niche' in Cleveland yet. And they were struggling to make ends meet.

Adele, who had been an accomplished sculptor in France, had assured the man at the Cheese shop that both she and Jacques would be there from opening to close, every day, if he would just give them a chance.

However, on that particular day, Jacques had been offered a unique opportunity to show his paintings to a downtown developer, who had expressed interest in purchasing a painting or two for a new office building.

What had started out to be only a few minutes late, quickly escalated into three hours.

"Well, what are you waiting for?" Kelly stood there, impatiently.

144

Katie wiped her hands on the front of her apron and approached him. He arranged seven different slivers on the counter. "Close your eyes."

Katie stared back at him, her heart pounding.

"I said close your eyes – I will *prove* you know nothing about cheese."

Adele's eyes welled. Katie shrugged and closed her eyes.

"Now, tell me the names of each one." He handed a piece to her."

First, she smelled it. Then, she ran her fingers over the surface. And finally, she tasted it."

Katie crinkled her nose. "Cheddar. No – English Cheddar." She grinned, still blindfolded. "Quite aged, I might add."

Kelly forced the breath out of his nostrils, like a child who was about to fly into a tantrum. "Lucky guess." He gave her another, softer variety.

Katie sniffed it. Her heart rate settled down and she smiled. She didn't need to touch it, or taste it. She got it right, as she did for the remaining five slivers. She popped her eyes open and grinned.

*Aunt Rose told me that helping Tyler at the cheese shop would someday pay off.*

Mr. Kelly blew out a frustrated breath. "Very well. But just one mistake and you will all be gone!"

Adele worked alongside Katie, watching out of the corner of one eye, amazed, as she not only held her own with the customers, she actually seemed to be extremely knowledgeable.

About twenty minutes after Katie began working, the man returned, determined to expose her as the fraud she was. He stood from across the way, watching her.

On the surface, things seemed to be going well. She engaged in conversation with his customers with ease. But when he observed Katie returning a wedge of cheese back to the case, after one of his loyal customers handed it back to her, he became enraged.

*What did this woman say to the man to make him change his mind and decide not to purchase the cheese?*

"Just what do you think you are doing, filling my customers with your nonsense?"

"I simply changed his mind."

"That's not the point."

"It's *precisely* the point." She grinned back at him, calmly, while wrapping a larger wedge of a different variety. She held it over the case to the customer. "When he told me why he was buying cheese today, I simply suggested a different variety."

*Thank you, Tyler.*

"What's so different about that cheese?" he asked in a voice steeped with skepticism.

"I beg your pardon sir, but if you truly knew half as much as you should about cheese, you would know that."

He was at a loss for words.

"Now then, I believe I've put in a fair hours' work, sir. I'll be on my way now." She smiled sweetly, handed Kelly her apron and left him standing there, looking lost.

As Katie gestured for Adele to follow her, she said a silent prayer of thanks.

"Oooh," Mrs. Kelly cooed, as she approached her husband's cheese shop from around the corner. "What did she buy, Joseph?"

He gave her a puzzled look. "Who?"

His wife pointed at the two women walking away from the store. "Mrs. Stockton - the captain's wife."

Mr. Kelly skidded to a halt and made a guilty face.

✲✩✦✲✩✲✩✩✦✩✦✩✲

Jacques still hadn't shown up. Katie offered Adele a ride home. Adele thanked Katie profusely and they began talking – becoming friends.

As they walked through the market to the car, Katie noticed several young children, unattended, wandering through the market. Two of them weren't wearing shoes, which got her attention.

*Who sends a child out to play without proper clothing and shoes?*

Adele told Katie the story behind the children – It saddened her. She returned to the market and convinced three market proprietors to open back up, long enough to allow her to purchase food for the children.

146

Adele knew where the children lived and they drove to the neighborhood. Katie didn't want to frighten the children, so, since they had seen Adele before, she asked Adele to take the packages to the door of the house. Katie watched from the car.

"Bless their hearts," she said aloud. She had seen enough. She had to do something.

Katie delivered Adele home, which was not far from where the children and their families lived. Through conversation, Katie also discovered that Adele was an artist herself – a sculptor. Adele offered to show Katie some of her work.

Katie loved it; she admired Adele. When she found out they hadn't found a permanent place to live yet, she got an idea. John had recently purchased property with a cottage, just down the street from their house. She planned to ask him if he had rented it out yet, as soon as he arrived back home next week, from the voyage he was currently on.

※ ※ ※ ※ ※ ※ ※ ※ ※ ※ ※ ※

After they had eaten supper on the evening of his return, and John had answered all of Katie's questions about his travels, it was time to turn in for the night.

John seized his jacket in one hand, her hand in the other and they ascended the stairs to turn in for the evening.

They had a brief conversation about Katie's escapades of the past weeks. But she was far too preoccupied to stay on task for long. John yawned and slid under the covers, ready to fall sound asleep … while Katie prepared to ask him her question.

She pulled on her cotton nightgown and snuggled up to him, breathing in his scent. Just as his eyes drooped, Katie propped herself up on her elbow and stared at him, causing his eyes to fly back open. Then Katie pressed her lips shut before launching into the pitch.

John half-listened to her story about the two young artists from France who needed a place to live, and how much Katie adored Adele. Katie had felt a spark of kinship with Adele; the very idea of a friend brought light to her face.

She could have asked him for a million dollars; he would have given it to her. But, fortunately for John, Katie settled for the little French chocolate box cottage, two doors down.

## ~ Thirty-Seven ~

HE STOPPED THE ENGINE at the curb, in front of the building. The car came to a jerking halt. When she opened the car door, John leaned over and stared up at the humble structure.

"Are you sure you have the right address, Katie?"

"Yes, this is it." She smiled back at him. "I'm sure it's not as bad as it looks from here, John, and the children are well cared for."

"How many children are there, for goodness sake?" He asked.

"There are at least eight." She lifted a basket from the back of the car and she let out a sigh. "But I'm not sure how many of them belong to which family. For the most part, I suspect that they are living alone." She sighed and closed the car door.

John gave her a look of astonishment. "How can that be? Where are their parents?"

"Their parents work very hard, long hours to support them. Adele says they try to stagger their hours but most of the time, their schedules keep them away from the children during their waking hours."

John began to show signs of restlessness.

Katie leaned back into the car. "They are good parents. Adele talks to them often. They know I am stopping by. I just want to see what the situation is, for now." Just before she turned to walk away, she said, "John, you don't need to stay. I will find a telephone and call for a taxi when I am ready to come home."

149

He didn't share her enthusiasm. "I will wait right here for you. And mind you, I am thinking twice about you coming here by yourself while I am away." John got out and leaned against the front fender, surveying the surroundings. He reached into his pocket and pulled out a stick of gum. He shoved it into his mouth and chewed on it while he waited for Katie to come back out.

Little faces, too many for John to count at the time, stared out at him from a dirty window.

Katie rolled her sleeves up as she entered the house to take a look around. There were blankets on the floor – she supposed they were a substitute for beds. The plaster was falling off the walls in places, exposing the raw lathe.

Katie's gaze drifted over to a window that faced the alley. It was broken and had been boarded up to keep out the November chill of Cleveland.

"You brought us bread and milk. And apples." The little girl, Nellie, squeezed Katie's hands as she peered deeper into the basket. "Did you bring me flowers, too?"

A deep ache filled Katie's heart as she watched the delighted little child revel in the glory of her simple gesture. She opened the basket and carefully removed the roses. She sat on one of the wooden crates and told her, "Roses are my favorite flower."

"In the whole world?"

She smiled. "Yes, in the whole world." Then she held a stem up to the light and explained further. "But you must handle most roses very carefully, because they have prickly things, called thorns. This is a special wild rose – one that doesn't have very many thorns."

The four-year-old little girl's eyes nearly doubled in size.

Outside, John carefully inched closer to the side of the house and peered through the window. Pleased that he had not been detected, he leaned in and watched Katie playing a game with the children to get them to eat. The laughter coming from inside the house was contagious. He felt a smile creep across his own face as he watched her juggle three apples at one time.

John abruptly stood. He rushed back to the car at the curb, staring down at his watch and wondered. Would there be enough time?

Katie looked around the room and announced, "I think it's about bed time. I've filled the basin with bathing water. Shall I count to ten?"

They groaned, but Katie knew just what was needed to convince them. She picked up a book she had seen earlier, turned away from them and smiled. "Alright then …" She quickly spun around and faced the children again. "Who wants to hear a story?"

Within fifteen seconds, there was a mad scramble to the basin. Katie giggled as she tidied up the scattered things around the room. The children snuggled into the pile of blankets. Katie sat next to them and began reading, until the last of them had fallen asleep.

Being read to always equaled love in Katie's mind. She drew in a deep breath, and then used the air to extinguish the lantern.

John had dozed off, but hastily jumped out and ran to the passenger door when he saw Katie step onto the curb, across the street from the house. When she approached the car, she noticed that there were sacks, tied together with string, laying in the back seat that hadn't been there earlier.

She was also aware that he wasn't smiling.

As he closed the car door for her, she turned to face him. "John – I am sorry if I've upset you. But, don't you see?"

"See what, Katie?" he asked as he positioned himself behind the steering wheel. She could sense frustration growing in his voice by the second.

She touched his sleeve, and in a voice filled with passion, she said, "You have purpose, John. And you have a passion in life."

"I have you – you are all I need."

"That's not true, John. There's more to life and you know it." His eyes caught the light in hers. "I know you love me. But I also know that the Great Lakes and the seas run through your veins."

"Katie, my dear …" he tried to jump in, but she rolled right over him and went on.

"Perhaps this is my purpose, John. Maybe this is my chance to help people help themselves." She looked straight ahead.

John's facial expression went quickly from frustration to amusement. He put his arm across her seat and turned his head toward the back. "Well, aren't you going to ask me?"

Her voice became quiet. Her eyes shifted. "Ask you what?"

"Aren't you just a little curious where these sacks came from?"

Peeking from the top of one of the bags was a metal bucket, holding two tiny shovels, and a pair of gloves. Katie jumped up on her knees and leaned over the seat. Her smile was unstoppable.

Another bag, filled to the brim with small pots, was topped off with a wide- brimmed, straw hat. And finally, she realized that the last bag had been responsible for the earthy, but sweet smell that filled the interior of the car.

John grinned. "Roses. And dirt. Although we have plenty of dirt at home, I suspected that you would be wanting this special mix."

She had opened her eyes at dawn, unable to go back to sleep. Katie's mind was filled with ideas. The supplies John had bought her were more than enough to get her started.

Katie moved seven pots of dirt to the ground and began to wash the soapstone bench. She looked up to find the captain standing in front of her.

"Well, don't just stand there," she smirked. "Would you like me to show you how it's done?" John smiled as she placed his hand around the trowel, and then put hers on top, and together they flipped the tip out of the dirt, excavating a perfectly round hole about three inches deep. Then they both scraped the loose dirt back around the pink rose vine and pressed it down.

"You must be careful not to pack the soil too tightly. The shoots are delicate and need to breathe." Then she looked up and him. He was wearing a silly grin." She giggled. "What are you thinking about?"

John had come to love watching Katie's face as she thought things through, the flash of insight in her eyes, the doubt twisting her lips and the glow of delight when she found a practical solution. He was proud of her.

"Have I ever told you how happy you've made me, my dear?"

# ~ Thirty-Eight ~

*November, 1915*

ON THE DAY William Stockton left Ireland to head off to war, Katie stood next to John on the platform of the train depot. Although tears streamed down Katie's cheeks and John put on his brave-face, their hearts swelled with pride as they observed the men of Quinn's Harbor, marching off to fight for the future of the world.

John watched in silence as his baby brother, in his new uniform, with its brass buttons shimmering in the sunlight, boarded the train.

At the top of the steps, Will turned back to them and smiled.

* * *

Shots from nearby shattered the sudden silence. The figure was in obvious pain. Will rushed to the downed soldier and knelt beside him. Wedging his arm beneath the soldier's shoulders and head, he desperately examined his face for some sign of life. Showers of earth rained down on them, each blast feeling closer than the last.

"You're hit," Will said as he hastily tore open the front of his binding uniform jacket. He knew immediately that it was bad. The young man winced, but did not struggle as Will attempted to tend to his wound. "It's probably just a flesh wound." Will said as he cradled him.

But they both knew that was not the case.

The young warrior grabbed Will's forearm, opened his mouth and tried to speak. He took his final breath as the light in his eyes faded. Will closed them with his thumbs and wiped away a tear that had escaped.

From across the trench, Will heard voices, hollering – warning him again. "Lieutenant! Have you lost your mind?" Gunfire erupted again, surrounding him.

The shrill sound of the captain's whistle was barely audible as the heavy guns continued to roar. "Get the hell out of there! *That's an order!"*

Will dragged his fallen comrade behind him, through the mud.

Another soldier went down. Will released the first one, and caught the fifteen-year-old boy from Dublin by the sleeve. He pivoted, retrieved the first soldier, and headed for the trench.

But he wasn't fast enough. He was only 20 feet from his unit when he was shot in both the leg and shoulder. Somehow, Will managed to drag himself, the lifeless body and the injured boy back to the trench.

## ~ *Thirty-Nine* ~

*October, 1916*

THE SNOW CAME EARLY, as forecasted, but not in heavy drifts; it floated down delicately for hours, soft and light as though spun from crystal.

John was sitting in the living room, making an entry in his journal, when he suddenly jumped up and darted out into the foyer. Then he froze in place. He felt himself turn pale - as white as his starched shirt.

Katie had been in the room and ran after him. Her eyes widened when she saw her husband's face.

"Will's badly injured."

She touched his sleeve. "John, no he isn't, silly. He's on his way home."

"He's not coming home." Then he turned to face her. "Not for a long time."

She ran to the table and pulled out the letter they had received earlier in the week from Will. She unfolded the paper and held it out to John. "He says in this letter that it won't be long. John, he will be home very soon."

But John knew better. Something was wrong; something was very wrong. That connection he and Will had; the same one their father and uncle had – it never lied. If someone kicked his uncle in the shin, his father felt the pain.

John tenderly kissed Katie. He gently handed his journal to her, spared her a brief, anguished glance before slowly climbing the staircase and opening the door to the library. He turned in place, looking down at her from the landing, expressionless. She clutched the journal to her chest with both hands and gazed back.

Katie wanted to follow him, but she knew that John wanted to be alone. She heard the library doors close.

Later, Katie stood in the open doorway of the library. When she saw John holding the wooden star Will had given him so long ago, she knew he was right. Will was not on his way home.

"Oh no," Katie whispered in the hallway. "Please, God, keep our Will safe."

John saw her and quickly pulled her into an embrace, gently rocking her as he felt her begin to crumble. "Why must we do this, John?"

She sobbed. "War is so horrible. It leaves us with so many ghosts."

He whispered against her cheek, but it couldn't blot the image from her mind. He pulled back slightly and gazed in her eyes. He guided her to a chair and he reeled to the window. It hurt too much to let her see the worry on his own face.

## ~ Forty ~

*February, 1917*

EXCEPT FOR THE PINES, the trees had shed their leaves for winter. The house was buzzing with activity in anticipation of Will's arrival. Although it was well into the month of February, the streets of downtown were still decorated with pine wreaths and red bows.

It had been cold enough to freeze the water in the birdbath in the courtyard, but the slight thaw the evening before had warmed the air enough to coax it to re-liquefy.

John had made arrangements for Will to move in with them; something that Will protested, but once he was assured that it was only temporary, until he was well enough to return to his home and the observatory in Ireland, he reluctantly agreed.

Katie stared down the track while John paced back and forth, as they waited.

Since the track curved in and out through the houses and buildings on its approach to the city, they couldn't see or hear the train quite yet. But John had already spotted the engine's puffs of smoke far beyond the river. It probably wouldn't be there for at least ten minutes.

There would always be a special place in Katie's heart for Will. She relived the afternoon he came to visit her; the day he dropped her into the horse's trough. She smiled and laughed to herself. Will had always known what she needed; he always had her best interest at heart.

The deep whistle of the train brought her back to the platform, awakening her from the daydream. The engine appeared from beyond the curve, huffing out extra steam as it slowed down, approaching the station. It glistened in the peaceful snowfall.

A blast of steam roared out from under the wheels. A conductor in a black uniform swung down to the platform and placed an iron stepping stool in front of the door on the fourth car.

Katie's heart skipped – she grabbed John's arm at her first glimpse of Will. He limped down the steps from the car, with a vacant expression.

As soon as she recognized Will, Katie ran to him, enveloping him in an embrace. But instead of the bear hug she had anticipated, he circled one arm around her and patted her back gently. She searched his face for some kind of light, but Will's eyes were hollow.

"Will, "John said as he embraced him, "I am so proud of you – you are a hero."

⋆ ⋆ ⋆ ⋆ ⋆ ⋆ ⋆ ⋆ ⋆ ⋆ ⋆ ⋆ ⋆

William irritably flinched, and then he lost his balance, falling back against the doorframe. John steadied his brother. Will pulled his arm loose and pointed a finger at him.

"I have seen the remains of my friends that no longer resembled a human being." He tasted the bile rising in his throat. "And I still hear the wretched, disbelieving screams of those who God unmercifully didn't claim immediately." He turned away from them.

John rubbed his face. He should have known this was coming. Katie reached out and touched his arm. Will shook it off and faced them again.

Will felt as though he had been trapped in a nightmare he would never awaken from. His face twisted in pain as his voice grew louder. "How can you all stand there and tell me I am a hero? And you want to …" He ran his fingers through his hair. "… *celebrate?*"

158

It took some doing, but Katie and John convinced Will to agree to go through with the celebration. They planned it for Friday, almost three weeks after his arrival in Cleveland.

It was a gloomy day for a celebration. February in Cleveland, complete with ice crystals nipping at cheeks and noses, left something to be desired, but even the weather couldn't stop how proud they were. William Stockton was a hero.

Just before their guests began to arrive, Katie sat by Will and took his hand. "I wish I could erase everything that happened to you. I wish the war had never happened at all."

Will stood and faced the window. An uncomfortable stiffness enveloped him.

She could tell that he was only half-listening. "But, because of you, there are many men who were able to return home and go on with their lives." Her heart broke for him and she squeezed his hand.

A quiet knock at the door interrupted her. Katie stood and moved to one side.

William's mouth dropped open as the drawing room doors parted slowly, revealing three young men standing in the foyer; faces he instinctively recognized. It took a little more time, but within a couple of minutes, he said their names aloud.

"Lawrence? Daniel? Gus?"

They saluted him. Gus stepped forward first. He motioned toward the doorway, where he saw Katie nod. A young woman with a little girl joined him.

"Lieutenant Stockton - I'd like you to meet my wife, Megan." His wife smiled and took Will's hand. Gus reached down and scooped up his little girl with his one arm. The two-year-old held out her arms to Will, as if she wanted to go to him.

Life slowly began seeping back into Will's face. He smiled. "And who might you be?"

The giggling mass of curly blond hair wiggled out of her father's arm and back to the floor, where she proudly announced, "Maryanne – and I'm two!"

Will squatted to her eye level and winked. "Well, Maryanne, I'll bet Miss Katie can find the perfect cookie, just for you!"

Katie took her by the hand and off to the kitchen.

When Will stood, Megan fell into his arms, catching him off-guard. In a charming Irish lilt, she said, "I can't begin to thank you for taking care of Gus. If it hadn't been for you, Maryanne would have lost her father and I would have lost my husband." Tears filled her eyes.

Gus gently guided Megan away from Will and out into the hallway.

Lawrence hobbled toward William. "Sir, I am here to personally invite you to my wedding, next month." He grinned. "She's from Chicago!"

Will caught his eye with a sly grin. "Why, Larry - you old dog, you!" He reached out and shook Lawrence's hand with a firm grip. "Just try to keep me away!"

He turned back to the doorway and studied the third young man, Daniel, standing alone, in silence. Nothing could ever change the bond William had with Daniel during those long months.

Lying about his birthday, Daniel had enlisted in the army at the age of fifteen. From the very beginning, Will had sensed that something wasn't right; there were too many times he had seen the boy in profile, gun in hand, where his instincts told him the lad couldn't be more than sixteen. Nevertheless, Danny did his job, just as well as any eighteen, or twenty, or twenty-five-year old would have.

Will always kept an extra eye out for the boy. Ironically, Danny had been the one who may have saved Will's life, on his very first day in the trench, bravely creating a diversion, giving Will enough time to evade capture.

Will approached Daniel and he smiled. "Danny, I do hope you are here to tell me you are taking me up on the offer to study with me at the observatory. We need good men like you."

The boy's face lit up, and he ran to Will. "Sir, I would be honored."

They hugged; Will pulled back and he studied his face. Then he rubbed the boy's chin roughly. "When did you get old enough to grow a beard, son?"

The doorbell rang. And the celebration was on.

## Forty-One

*September, 1918*

WILL SPENT MUCH of his time recuperating by the lake, building castles in the Edgewater sand. Not only was it therapeutic, he had become quite good at it.

Katie joined him one afternoon that fall. "We're going to miss you, William. Are you sure you won't stay here with us?"

"If I am to avoid falling down into a bit of a *rabbit hole*, I feel the need to return to my life and to my work at the observatory." He trickled water from the pail around the perimeter of the structure, creating a moat. "I have been here for more than a year now. If I stay much longer, I'm afraid I will continue to do nothing more than this."

"Doesn't building sand castles make you happy?" Katie asked Will.

He shrugged. "Not unless I can build them in the sky."

~ *Forty-Two* ~

*December, 1920*

KATIE PEEKED THROUGH the leaded glass on the door and ran to the hall mirror to take a glance at her appearance.

He was home. The house would be filled with laughter and joy once again. Katie flung open the front door just as he had laid down several boxes, reaching for the doorknob.

There he stood. Katie smiled and she caught her breath. Beneath the five-day beard, John's lips formed a captivating pirate's smile. Katie had mentioned to him at the end of a previous voyage that she loved being surprised by which John Stockton would greet her each time he returned home.

He smelled of sun, salt, and man. John smoothed her palm against his beard. Then he kissed the galloping pulse beneath her delicate wrist. He dropped his mouth to hers. "I've missed you so, Katie."

He leaned slightly back toward the foyer and snagged a linen bag from the top of one of the boxes. He held it out to her.

In the sack was a layer of sweet-smelling flower-shaped soaps. She smiled and cooed at John as she inhaled the delicious fragrance.

"Oooh …"

He grinned back at Katie, and stepped out into the foyer. He returned with a much larger package. "But this, my dear, is something I knew belonged to you the moment I saw it in the shop."

Katie was like a little girl in a candy store. She eagerly untied the ribbon and unwrapped the package. The first thing she saw was a sea of blue. She dropped the package to the floor and unfolded yards and yards of the most exquisite sapphire blue damask fabric she had ever seen. She ran to the window seat, the fabric unfolding as she moved, and held it against the upholstered cushions. She gave John a grin. He nodded in agreement.

She lovingly tucked the fabric around the cushions and stood back. "Look – It reflects the beauty of the lake! Oh John, it's exactly what I had envisioned for proper cushions! It's magnificent!" She threw her arms around him and kissed him on the cheek.

A sizzle of excitement raced through his body. He whispered in her ear, "My sweet Katie, I have one more thing for you."

She pulled back slightly and her eyes lit up. "Roses?"

"Roses aren't quite what I had in mind," he said as he pulled her close. He inhaled deeply. Her hair smelled like lilacs and vanilla. "But that will have to wait."

Katie followed John out into the foyer, where he picked up a narrow box and handed it to her. When she started pulling on the string holding the paper together, he stopped her. "Not yet, my dear." He picked up the large crate and motioned with his head for her to follow him out the kitchen door. "Come with me."

A full moon hung high in the sky, creating long shadows across the driveway and front lawn. When they reached the attic, John began unpacking the crate, and Katie found herself drawn to the window.

"Almost finished," she heard John say. Katie turned around to see John bringing out a large, brass cylinder in her direction.

"This looks much like the telescope Will has at home." Katie had seen Will use a huge one at the observatory, as well.

He nodded. "Your box has the stand. Open it."

Katie lifted the top off the box and pulled out the sections that eventually pieced together a tripod for the telescope. John placed it on the tripod, securing it with several twists of his wrist.

He straightened and grinned at Katie. She joined him at the window. Lights dotted the horizon, like little lanterns, in the middle of the dark purple sky.

"The water – and the sky … There is so much - everywhere I look. How will I know where to look? Who I am looking at?"

She watched as he made adjustments, sliding crystal disks in and around behind the lens. When he'd positioned everything just as he wanted it, he stepped back and motioned for Katie to step up to the eyepiece. "Have a look."

Katie was silent. After a minute, she moved away, then she returned her eye to the apparatus. Thoroughly exasperated, finding herself staring out at a small patch of dark sky, she blew out a sigh. "It's no use." She stood. "I can't see anything, John." Not daring to move the telescope, for fear that she might lose any slim chance to catch a glimpse of what John saw, she walked to the window. She was thoroughly frustrated.

A brief twinkle lit his eyes again. He manipulated the moving mechanism so that it pointed to a freighter out on the lake. John adjusted a dial on the telescope.

"Will says he uses his to study the constellations," she said, her eyes still fixed on the lake.

John chuckled and placed his hands on Katie's hips, guiding her back to the instrument. "Will knew more about the constellations, when he was a child, than the great astronomers did."

"Did you bring this so I could study the constellations?"

His eyes narrowed. "Not exactly." He switched off the electric light and returned to Katie's side at the telescope.

His breath tickled her ear as he bent to kiss her cheek. "Any time you feel lonely for me, you can come up to the attic and view the very same thing I am seeing."

She smiled. "So we will be together?"

"And it can also serve as a reminder that, when problems, such as loneliness, seem larger than life, a telescope has the power to help you see past yourself."

## ~ Forty-Three ~

**"I HATE IT!"**

"Kathleen Stockton – stop squirming so! Be still."

Abigail turned her around and attempted to fasten the side buttons, but Katie shooed her hands. Abigail persisted, fussing as the captain's wife slapped her fingers away like a pesky swarm of fruit flies.

**"NO!"**

A dress so extravagant made her uncomfortable. Besides, it *was* uncomfortable. Mrs. Simpson almost pounced, pointing one finger accusingly at Katie. Then she took hold of her upper arms.

"Dear, you may not be used to playing the part of a lady back in *Fin's Wharf*, or wherever it is you are from. But Captain Stockton deserves a proper lady at his side."

The implication wasn't lost on Katie. She frowned. A stray tress had worked itself loose from her combs, and Mrs. Simpson tried in vain to tuck it back into place. "Kathleen, you've been married for eight years. Don't you think it's time you stop behaving like a child?"

The tight, beaded, high neckline choked Katie as she scratched at the heavily embellished, prickly gown.

Abigail Simpson had selected it for Katie Stockton's portrait while on a recent trip to Paris. And she hadn't stopped bragging about it to the community since the day she had returned to Cleveland. The dress arrived a week later and she could not wait to show it off.

Her eyes glared with triumph as she stood back after fastening the final hook on the gown. Mrs. Simpson practically shimmied with glee.

Katie turned away, panting, while she tugged at the collar. The arrogant Abigail Simpson, with all her sophistication and power, never ceased to intimidate her.

John heard the commotion as Katie fled the bedroom, taking flight down the stairs, her fists full of taffeta. She darted into the living room and slammed the doors before Mrs. Simpson could catch up to her. He stopped outside the door and knocked.

"Katie – is everything alright?"

"No, it's not." she said, whispering through quiet sobs. John slowly opened the door and found her sitting on the floor. She chewed her lip as her eyes met his.

He approached her with a smile and he held out his hands to help her stand. John had only recently returned to Cleveland himself, and he was unaware that Katie hadn't been consulted or permitted to pick out what she wanted to wear for the sitting – he understood her, and would have known that this gown was not suited to her.

Intrigued by the sight of Katie tied into such a stiff, fussy, *straight jacket* of a gown, he reached out and lifted her face. "Why the tears, Katie?"

Mrs. Simpson entered the room, out of breath.

Katie threw her arms around John's neck. Her breath warmed his chest with whispered urgency. "Please – do I have to wear this dress for my portrait?"

John smiled. He gently eased her off his chest and shook his head. "Why would you think you have to wear this garment for the sitting?"

Mrs. Simpson jumped in, arguing, trying to make it sound as though Katie was unappreciative; incorrigible - like a spoiled child. Katie's expression changed from sadness to rage at the insinuation.

John tried to keep from laughing, knowing his wife was anything but spoiled. He faced Mrs. Simpson and addressed her.

"Thank you Mrs. Simpson. But for the portrait, Katie will make her own selection."

Katie gave Abigail a glare that could have stopped traffic.

With what she viewed as the captain's permission, Katie ripped off the gown and tossed it, aimlessly, as hard as she could across the room. The frock landed on Mrs. Simpson; the heavy beading and metal stays weighed her down, causing her knees to buckle. Abigail, surprised and insulted, balled the gown up and stared, unable to move.

Dressed only in her undergarments, Katie shivered in the chill of the evening, her eyes searching the room. She impulsively grabbed the blue damask fabric laying across the window seat cushion and enveloped herself in the soft fabric. Katie studied the sapphire blue pattern and thought about how it made her feel warm … and safe.

She got a glint in her eyes; John saw it immediately. She raised her chin, part anxiety, part defiance.

With the knowledge that once the snowball started rolling with her, it would only grow, he felt a reluctant smile creep across his face.

And he waited.

Before Abigail, or John for that matter, could stop her, Katie had stripped completely naked, down to her bare skin, and draped herself loosely in the fabric, holding it up, barely covering her breasts.

The words came to her as if somebody had just breathed them into her ear. "There! *This* is what I want to wear for the portrait!"

## Forty-Four

*"HUMPH!"* Her eyebrows arched. She faced John. "Why **...**" she sputtered. *"I never! ..."* Mrs. Simpson was fuming.

An amused look crossed his face. His eyes twinkled at her.

"Abigail, I am quite convinced you never have – but that's a conversation you must have with your gentleman callers. He quirked his eyebrows in amusement. "I'm afraid I can't fix that."

The cracks in Mrs. Simpson's face hardened. She realized her mouth was hanging open and shut it. Her lips thinned and curved downward; her forehead crinkled in bewilderment.

*        *     *   *  * *

John returned to the living room after seeing Abigail to the door. Katie, still holding tight to the sea of blue fabric, was facing the window looking down, disappointed that she had spoken out loud to Abigail in that way. She glanced over and caught him staring at her.

To hide her blush, Katie pulled the fabric tighter around her shoulders. "I'm afraid Mrs. Simpson left rather abruptly," Katie said in a voice filled with remorse. She bit her lip and swallowed hard.

John pulled her close. "She did seem a bit unhappy, didn't she?" He grinned. "In a snit, you might say."

Still, she frowned. "I seem to have complicated your life." Katie tried to push back the emotions building inside her.

"Katie, my dear, you should know by now how you have brought light into my world."

"Even if I don't exactly fit? ... the odd-shaped puzzle piece?" Katie asked with a pout. She walked to the window and touched the lamp on the ledge. "I feel like this oil lamp, in this house of electric lights."

John pulled her close. "Katie, my dear, you *are* my world." He crossed the room and switched off the electric light. Then he returned to the window and gently lifted the lamp. "And I will always prefer this oil lamp to the house of electric lights." He set the lamp back in its place.

John moved his finger along the folds of fabric draped around her. "And I searched a very long time to find you ... the perfect, final piece of the puzzle."

The hurricane lamp flickered on the ledge at the center of the window. She watched their whirling, flickering shadows as they danced to the music of their hearts. Before long, Katie had dropped the fabric into a pile on the floor and the flame had extinguished.

And what followed, illuminated by the moonlight streaming in through the misty panes of the window, only Lake Erie knows.

~ *Forty-Five* ~

*February, 1921*

KATIE CLENCHED THE leather hand strap, as she stood in the streetcar, agonizing over the possible reasons she had been summoned to the home. What happened? More sickness? Or worse – death?

The first thing that caught her attention was the sign pinned on the door as she approached the porch. She ignored it and knocked on the door. An upstairs window opened slightly and she strained to hear the voice.

"I'm sorry, ma'am, but as you can see, we may be under quarantine very soon."

Katie's face buckled and she covered her eyes with her hand. "May I please come inside?"

The woman hesitated, then she blew out a puff of frustration. "You understand you will be putting yourself at risk."

Sitting beside Nellie's bed, Katie twisted a damp handkerchief between her fingers. The little girl's temperature had refused to drop, no matter how many times she bathed her face. She did not recognize Katie at all. "Please get better, Nellie," she sighed, fighting back tears of helplessness.

Katie had been so worried about Nellie that it was beginning to affect her spirit. And that concerned John.

About a week following Nellie's recovery, John returned early from the office, to find Katie dozing in a living room chair.

It was bad enough that his travel schedule hadn't allowed him much time at home in Cleveland with her, but the past few days had him keeping especially late hours at the office, sometimes until after midnight.

He didn't want to disturb her; she had been working so hard, between the families and taking care of her roses. She sensed his presence and she opened her eyes.

He gently pulled her out of her chair. "I know I have been spending a lot of time at the office. And it seems like I am neglecting you."

"Oh, John – you know I don't think that. I know how important your work is to you."

"I am also aware that I am not the only one with important work." He took her hand. "I have been working on a special business deal. And I am ready to share it with you."

She tilted her head to one side. He reached inside his coat and brought out an envelope, thick with folded documents. After he opened the envelope, he lifted the paper off the top and handed it to her.

Katie walked slowly around the room while she read the document, finally settling in front of the picture window. Her mouth dropped open.

"Now, Katie, you understand that it will be an ongoing quest to maintain the funding. And that it will require outside contributions as well."

She ran to him and threw herself into his arms so hard he stumbled backward a few steps. The document fell from her hands and floated, landing face up on the floor, the top line standing out in boldface print:

**The Stockton Foundation –
A Not-for-Profit Charity Organization**

~ *Forty-Six* ~

*March, 1921*

KATIE FRETTED FOR WEEKS over the things Mrs. Simpson had said to her. She felt as though the woman was predisposed to hate anything she liked. However, she knew that if she gave the slightest indication that it bothered her, John would step in and take matters into his own hands. And that wasn't the answer.

She inhaled a deep breath as she sorted through the morning mail. An especially ornate envelope, slightly larger than the rest in the pile, kept peeking out at the edges, begging for her attention. She ran the letter opener along the crease, popping off the seal at the top, and pulled out the contents.

It was an invitation; a request for them to attend the dedication for a newly completed arcade; a vaudeville and silent film house, just around the corner from them. Katie smiled. She already loved everything about Gordon Square – this only imbedded it deeper in her heart.

Katie opened the next envelope and removed a card. Her eyes scanned past the greeting and dropped straight to the bottom of the card. They were also being invited to a party following the screening of the movie. Her heart skipped a beat. The party was being hosted by Abigail Simpson.

April was barely one month away. Katie continued reading as she walked to the pantry and made a mark on the wall calendar.

☆₊⁕ ⁕⁕₊ ⋆ ⁕ ⋆⁕⁕ ⁕⁕

Despite the weather, the energy was electric; excitement and anticipation filled the air. Hundreds of people had gathered at West 65th Street and Detroit Avenue for the event. Even the rain couldn't put a damper on the enthusiasm of the crowd.

The new motion picture theater was the centerpiece of Gordon Square. The landmark would surely put the area on the map, and keep it there. After a few speeches and a melody from the orchestra, the Capitol opened to the waiting crowd. John cupped Katie's elbow, guiding her to take in the beautiful theater. She was mesmerized by the artisanship and detail that went into her surroundings.

A round, spoked fixture, outfitted with bare bulbs, overflowed with golden light, throwing shadows highlighting an intricately tinted theme of dusty rose and grey. Elaborately carved ivory colored wall medallions and plaster pillars further heightened the senses.

They were escorted past a decorative fireplace on the second floor mezzanine to the balcony, where they found their seats, on the aisle, a few rows from the front. Katie was pleased to see that they were seated next to one of John's architects, Timothy Mason, along with his wife and their beautiful daughter, Julia.

The heavy curtain masking the stage, parted slowly as the lighting dimmed.

But not before Katie was distracted by a flash of red hair a few rows from the front, on the main floor. Nearly 800 seats spanned out before her eyes on the main floor, and that seat was the one that got her attention. She wanted to dive under the seats in front of them. Mrs. Simpson was sitting with some of John's business associates and their wives.

Katie had ransacked her closet for something Mrs. Simpson would approve of, although she began second-guessing her decision the moment she saw the woman.

John gently took her hand and whispered, "Katie, I have no desire to attend the reception if you will be uncomfortable. I shall send our regrets with the Masons."

She bristled. "No, I will be fine. I can only imagine the stories she will be telling her friends about me ... her assaults on my sense of style." No matter what she tried on that night, she looked haphazard. At least to her, she did.

"If I may be perfectly honest with you, my dear -- I am rather fond of what you chose to wear for your portrait." He gave her hand a squeeze and smiled with a hunger that sent her heart into a wild dance.

"Stop saying that." She couldn't hide her smile.

John hung his head, but a mischievous smirk suggested otherwise.

Katie looked straight ahead, but whispered, "How can such a busybody have so many friends? I will never know what they are being told."

"They are all very much aware of the way Abigail operates. I suspect they have all had similar experiences with the woman. She's not as popular as you would think." He gave her a knowing wink. "Besides, after she makes you drink a cocktail of eye-of-newt, you won't even notice she's there."

As the music from the Wurlitzer serenaded the crowd, Katie all but forgot about Mrs. Simpson and her questionable intentions. John smiled throughout the movie, every time he heard Katie giggle, knowing she was thinking about his reference to Abigail being a witch.

"Oh, I think Agnes Ayers is beautiful, don't you?" Katie whispered to Julia as the screen lit up. The glamorous female lead glided across the screen in front of them. "I hear she is in a new film, called *The Sheik*, and her lover is Rudolph Valentino – can you imagine playing a love scene with *him*?"

"Maybe. But I *can't wait* until *next month*," Julia said, wistfully.

The fem fatale stopped and faced the camera, bathing the audience in a smoldering gaze, drawing quiet gasps from the female members of the audience. Following a crescendo flowing from the Wurlitzer, the scene vignetted, and then faded altogether.

A new hole revealed itself in the darkness on the screen and expanded into the next one.

"What's special about next month, Julia?" Their heads continued to lean together, whispering in private conversation for a few minutes, discussing an upcoming feature attraction. "But isn't that film about the battles of war?" Katie asked with a note of surprise in her voice.

"Mrs. Stockton," Julia squealed. "*He's* starring in that one! Have you ever seen anyone more handsome?" The man sitting behind them shushed her.

"Which one?" Katie whispered back. She glanced at Julia's face and saw that look; the look of a young woman, head-over-heels in love with a movie star.

"Why Howard, of course – the general! Who else?" Julia giggled. *Of course.*

The woman in the row in front of them turned around. *"Please! Do you mind?"*

Fortunately, for the people sitting around them, Katie skillfully maneuvered Julia to curtail any further comments until the first of several intermissions.

More beautiful faces appeared, flickering in the dark, filling out the remainder of the film, accompanied by dramatic music being piped from the stage, beneath the screen.

✦ ✦ ✦ ✦ ✦ ✦ ✦ ✦ ✦ ✦ ✦

Captain Stockton helped his wife with her wrap and handed it over to the maid. John whistled long and low. "You sure look like a movie star to me."

The slightest hint of a smile touched her face as she took in the sea of fashionable dresses surrounding her as they approached the second floor ballroom at the Simpson mansion. For awhile, she felt completely relaxed. But good things must always come to an end.

She tried not to let it show, but at the sound of Mrs. Simpson's voice, she grimaced. From behind, Katie could sense an intense analysis flaring at her from Mrs. Simpson.

John felt it as well. He slowly turned in Abigail's direction; he nodded and smiled when he caught her eye.

Abigail hastily set her plate down on a side table. Her expression relaxed as she wiped her fingers on a napkin before pressing it to her lips, and she continued moving through the crowd.

Katie was grateful to have Julia by her side as a diversion from Mrs. Simpson's presence. The young woman managed to steer the conversation around to the general, which got the attention of the men in the group. They immediately took over the discussion, transforming it into a review of a recent movie featuring *the general.*

Julia's brain carried her off to another world. Their voices became drone background noise as she replayed scenes from the last film starring her hero. "Don't you just wonder what he really sounds like?" Julia remarked, rather hastily, still in her fog.

Julia re-entered, with a thud, back into her own life as Katie gently shook her arm. It became quiet. They all stared at her.

Katie smiled. "Why, that's a very interesting question, Julia."

"I bet he has a deep, romantic voice." Julia blushed, covered her eyes with her hands and turned away.

The men laughed at her. "As long as he's on our side, leading our troops into battle, the general doesn't ever need to say a word."

Julia nodded, her face still covered. Katie cringed for her sake.

## ~ Forty-Seven ~

SHE DOWNED THE CONTENTS in the cup with three quick swallows, resulting in two spots of color appearing high on her cheeks.

John looked around through the gathering for Katie. Her laugh sailed out from across the floor and his eyes instinctively went to her. He did a double take. She was with Abigail Simpson and her friends.

Katie was indeed laughing with everyone else - only just a little louder than usual. He dropped his fork onto his plate, left it on a chair and slowly made his way through the crowd, reluctantly stopping two times for polite conversation.

John folded his arms and leaned forward, scrutinizing Katie. Then a smile creeped across his face. "You're tipsy."

Yes, she was. If he hadn't been worried that they were in the middle of prohibition or concerned she would become ill, he would have found the situation humorous. He caught her elbow, but she pushed him back, standing on her own.

Katie grinned and hiccupped. "Abigail gave me fruit punch." She hiccupped again. "With strawberries."

"Is that so ... How much?" John made eye contact with Abigail, who was already retreating into the crowd, the color draining from her cheeks.

"Just a cup." She sat down hard in an upright chair, then, as if she had suddenly remembered something, she stood up again. "Or ..." she paused, waving a finger as she continued. "Maybe two ..." Katie swooned.

John put his arm around her. She sank into him like a spoon into a mixing bowl of marshmallow icing.

He was absolutely furious with Mrs. Simpson. He caught her eye again, across the room. The woman's behavior was intolerable. Regardless of what Katie thought, he was going to have words with her, before he left on his next trip. And he didn't care *who* her connections were.

Abigail would surely try to talk her way out of it, as usual, but providing lame excuses after making John angry was like blowing your breath against a gale wind.

John put the car in gear, driving out onto the road and wove in and out of the streets back through town, in silence. Once they reached Edgewater, he began randomly spouting off. His eyes snapped with anger and his fists clenched. "I'm afraid Mrs. Simpson has finally met her match." He stepped on the brake at the stop sign.

Katie, who John thought had been sleeping, began giggling uncontrollably. She sat straight up. "Abigail and I had a nice, long talk tonight," she proudly proclaimed."

He gritted his teeth as he tried to cool his rising anger toward Mrs. Simpson. "I'm sure you did." What the hell did the woman think she was doing? He rubbed his knuckles in his open palm like a mortar in a pestle, in agitation, then eased up and hit the accelerator again.

"Abigail was trying very hard to get me to drink the punch. I think she was trying to get me drunk, and do something foolish ..."

John made a right turn onto Clifton and interrupted her. "I have a mind to have the woman arrested – for what, I'm not certain, but I'll think of something," he fumed.

However, Katie finished her sentence, as though John hadn't cut her off. "... so I had to prove she was wrong." She smiled.

"Katie ..."

"I may have had one or two ..." She held up three fingers and hesitated.

John interrupted her. *"Three?"* He could see the wide grin on her face in his peripheral vision.

"... but Mrs. Simpson had *four*."

He stopped the car and stared over at his wife, concern etching his face. Did he hear her right? Had Katie attempted to drink Abigail under the table? Doubt clogged his brain. He held her face in his hands, his gaze serious. "That was a very dangerous thing to do."

Katie responded with an impish grin.

"Sometimes you worry me. That was an awful lot of effort, just to make a senseless point, Katie. You know that drinking is against the law."

John had lost track of the times he had been approached to use one of his ships over the past year to transport illegal libations across the lake from Canada. Captain Stockton took his business very seriously, following the letter of the law and never even considered it. In his opinion, anyone who would do so was out of his mind. And even crazier were the hundreds of people who drove cars and trucks across Lake Erie to accomplish the feat when it froze over.

Katie tucked the corner of her mouth into a pout. John parked in the drive and turned the engine off. He helped Katie out of the car, one arm around her waist.

With an expression so sweet on her face, Katie fumbled with the drawstring, unable to open her bag. The more she tried, the more tangled up the string became. She gave him a look of exasperation and handed it over to John. "You open it."

He looked at her.

She said it again. "Open it, John."

John pulled the knots out of the cord and opened the little purse, holding it at bay. Inside, he saw a powder compact, some small folded papers and a few coins. He tilted his head in puzzlement and she laughed.

"Goodness – It's just a handbag, John! Nothing to be afraid of, silly!" She rolled her eyes and grabbed the bag. She fished inside and pulled out one of the papers.

Katie had discovered Abigail was made up of a combination of pieces from several different puzzles; nothing fit. Just as Katie felt sorry for the woman and was ready to forgive her for one slight, she found a new way to offend her.

And Katie was determined to outsmart her at her own game. She unfolded the paper and dangled it playfully in front of her face. John snatched it from her.

It was a check. Made out to The Stockton Foundation.

In the amount of *twenty-five thousand dollars*.

And it was signed by Mrs. Abigail Simpson.

"Well, I'll be damned." This time he didn't apologize for the language.

Katie was still tossing and turning long after John had fallen asleep. She stared over in amazement that, unlike herself, her husband could sleep through just about anything.

Watching John snooze like a baby was only making things worse, so she flung the quilt aside and sat up.

Still a little disoriented from the effects from the liquid refreshment of the evening, Katie opened the kitchen door and stepped out onto the driveway landing. She tiptoed out and drew in a deep breath.

Something was different in the air. She walked out onto the driveway and turned her attention to the carriage house. Katie smelled a cigarette, and turned to look.

At the corner of the carriage house was Adele, having a smoke. Adele's eyes met Katie's. "I'm sorry," Adele whispered softly, in between drags. "Jacques would have my hide if he knew I was smoking again." She inhaled deeply, her eyes closing as if reestablishing her strength.

"We all slip up now and again."

When Katie said that, Adele laughed so hard it turned into a cough. Katie patted her on the back.

Adele bit her lip to keep from huffing another nervous laugh. "I am quite good at *slipping up*, aren't I?" She threw the cigarette butt to the driveway and ground it into the pavement with her slipper.

Katie wasn't following Adele's line of thought, so she remained silent. Adele leaned against the door to the carriage house and let out a sigh.

"Have you ever felt as if you've made a mistake, but you can't do anything about it because you will ruin everyone else's lives?"

Katie leaned in. "Adele, you don't mean that."

"Maybe. But how will I ever know?" She slid her back down the door and sat on the pavement. "Jacques says it's time we have a child."

184

Katie joined her, sitting on the driveway, next to her. "Isn't that something you want as well?"

"Of course I want a family. I just don't know if this is the right time. There's so much I haven't done yet – and once I have a child, I will never travel again." She met Katie's eyes with an intensity that gave her chills. "I want to see more of the world – to meet and study with other artists."

For years, Adele had allowed herself to look into the future, picturing them, white-haired, traveling the globe together. But now when she looked into the future, she couldn't see anything at all. "I love Jacques; really I do," she said, wishing the emotion would come as easily as the words.

Katie put her arm across Adele's shoulders. "Tell Jacques that you need more time. I'm sure he will understand, Delly."

Adele stood and quietly said, "I've already had a few scares."

Katie's eyes found Adele's. "You mean …?"

She nodded her head slowly. "I went to the doctor. He said I am just very irregular. He says it can be controlled."

Katie, just over a whisper, said, "That's good."

Then Adele took Katie forcibly by the shoulders. "But, that's just it, Katie. I don't feel I have any control over my life."

# ~ Forty-Eight ~

KATIE FITTED THE sapphire blue Damask cushion into the window seat and took a few steps back. It was beautiful. "Mrs. Wiggs, it's lovely."

Mrs. Wiggs handed her the remaining fabric, wrapped in paper. "It is such a handsome fabric; such a shame you couldn't do something more with it."

For the longest time, Katie was afraid to make anything out of the fabric because it was so beautiful she couldn't bear to see it cut into pieces.

Katie had a sudden flashback; to the night she and Mrs. Simpson argued about her portrait sitting. She remembered how safe and warm the bolt of fabric felt as she wrapped herself in it.

She suddenly tore the paper off the package and unfolded the fabric. Was it possible? Would there be enough?

Mrs. Wiggs didn't wait for the question – she saw it in Katie's eyes. She quickly turned the fabric every-which-way, draping portions of it around Katie. She scribbled on a notepad in her purse.

The grin on Mrs. Wiggs' face spread over to Katie's face – she had her attention. She opened her case, rummaging through her sewing notions and held up an envelope. "Mrs. Stockton – how would you feel about a new party dress?"

Katie held her hand over her heart. "Do you think it's possible?"

Mrs. Wiggs let her creative juices flow. "I could use a dress I made for myself as a pattern and make it smaller to fit you." She stepped back and grinned at Katie. "Yes, I do believe we can make this work.

~ *Forty-Nine* ~

"I ENVY YOU SO, Delly," Katie said with a smile. "You have found a purpose for your life; something beautiful for others to enjoy."

Adele's smile turned from wistful to stern as she traced her finger along the edges of the clay spinning on the turntable. She took her foot off the pedal and spun around on the stool to face Katie.

"Kathleen Stockton – please don't tell me you think your life doesn't have purpose! Why, you have made such a difference in so many people's lives; people who had nothing before they met you." She clasped Katie's hands in hers. "The Stockton Foundation distributes food and warm clothing to so many ... and your plan to populate the community with your wild roses – a symbol of your undying love, is something I could only dream about."

Katie smiled. "I guess you're right. I just wish I could do more."

Later that evening she stood back in admiration after Jacques hung the new painting on the wall over the fireplace. A haunting, sorrowful stretch of Lake Erie winter coastline, streaked in blue, purples and stone gray, it took her breath away.

Katie placed her hand across her heart. "It's beautiful." She touched the luxurious gradations of paint, immersing herself in the textured layers on the canvas. "Jacques – why aren't you out there, sharing your talents with the world?"

He hung his head slightly. "Perhaps I am fearful."

"Fearful? Whatever for?"

"That I am not good enough to be a great artist."

"Rubbish," Katie said aloud, causing his head to pop up. She took Jacques' hand. "Jacques – are you afraid to fail?"

"What if I can't become a great painter …" his face darkened and he swallowed hard.

Katie met his eyes, interrupting Jacques' thoughts with a gentle smile and said, "If you don't make it as a painter, funnel that passion into something else." She squeezed his hand and went on. "Purpose is the reason you journey. Passion is the fire that lights your way." She grabbed a pencil and jotted the words on a piece of notepaper. "Here - just in case you forget." And she pushed it into his hand.

A slow smile lit Jacques' face. He had never been one to give up easily, and he was grateful that Katie had reminded him of that.

## ~ Fifty ~

SHE SAW SOMETHING OUTSIDE through the back yards; a shadow. Closer evaluation showed that it was Katie. But what was she doing out there, alone at night again? Adele turned her head, watching the white nightgown make its way back toward the house like a stealthy ghost.

This was the third time in a week she had seen Katie return to the house in the middle of the night. While it wasn't out of the ordinary for Adele to be up late, it wasn't like Katie at all.

Where had she been going? Adele was worried.

The next night, Adele camped out on the back porch, waiting to see what Katie was up to. She moved to a place in the side yard where she could be inconspicuous. And she waited.

She caught her first glimpse of Katie, at the edge of the courtyard. The moon was still high but just as Adele got Katie in her sights, a mass of dark clouds covered it, and she disappeared from sight, blending into the shadows of the willow tree,

Adele rushed to the front yard, where she could see Katie in the courtyard garden, lovingly plucking the dying brown roses from among the flourishing bright red buds. Adele breathed a sigh of relief that Katie hadn't strayed beyond her own yard.

"Katie," she whispered as she approached, watching her lean down to uproot yet another weed. There was no indication that Katie heard her, but she stood and hastily headed out front.

Adele followed Katie, heart in her throat, to the road, where she barely hesitated before she crossed the street and down the steps to the beach. And then she dropped out of sight. Adele sprinted to the ridge and peered over the edge.

Lightning bugs winking across the beach pointed the way while white breakers bashed themselves against the rocky overhanging at the base of the cliff.

There she was – wading in the shallow water of the lake. A twig cracked as Adele descended the stairs and took a step closer. She held her breath and then exhaled when she saw that Katie hadn't heard her. She watched her reach into the water for something.

Shells? Adele hadn't known Katie to be a shell collector. But even more perplexing - as Katie retrieved her treasures from the water, she appeared to be holding them up to the light before joyfully placing them in the gathered skirt of her nightgown. They were too small to be shells, but it was difficult for Adele to tell what they were, given her distance. Katie moved a little further, and then repeated her previous actions.

What was Katie collecting from under the surface of the lake?

"Katie," Adele said again.

Katie's eyes peered up at Adele, on the ridge, unblinking as if she didn't see her. The wind ballooned Katie's white nightgown, carrying Adele's voice away with it.

Of course! Katie was sleepwalking and she was completely unaware of what she was doing.

But why?

Adele followed Katie back to the house, where she opened the side door and closed it behind her. Adele returned to her own house, but tossed and turned for the remainder of the night.

## ~ Fifty-One ~

KATIE COULDN'T WAIT to get home. She had made a trip downtown, but it was not part of her weekly visit. She was a woman on a mission.

Adele had shared with her that she had been invited to participate in an art show, two weeks from the following Saturday night. Adele's sculptures were gaining attention and Jacques' paintings were already beginning to adorn walls in Cleveland. Katie had convinced Adele that this would be the perfect opportunity to get exposure.

Adele hadn't said it, but Katie knew that she hadn't bought a new dress in years. All she told Katie was that she might be unable to participate. However, Katie had her own suspicions.

Katie tried on dozens of dresses with accessories and, after two hours, she found seven that she thought would be perfect for Adele and she brought them home on approval.

Adele balked when Katie told her she had brought dresses home for herself, but was simply wondering how they would look on her. Claiming she didn't need a new dress, Adele turned to leave, but Katie begged her to go upstairs with her. Her mind was made up - they would both try them all on, and later, Katie would decide which would be her gift to Adele.

She crossed the room to open Katie's wardrobe. The light in Adele's eyes changed as they immediately settled on a red ensemble, then became distracted by a dusty rose two-piece suit.

While they tried on the dresses, Adele couldn't help noticing in the mirror that Katie was thinner than she should be. "You've lost weight. Maybe you're working too hard."

Katie laughed the comment off. "That's nonsense, Delly. If anything, I am not working hard enough!"

Her hair had become wild in the humid air off the lake, strongly resembling a cumulous auburn cloud of frizziness. She sighed as she scrutinized it in the mirror. She frowned and ran her fingers through it. Gripping the hairbrush on the nightstand tightly, she whisked it from the table and began fiercely brushing her long tresses. Katie sighed and surrendered the brush over to Adele, who always managed to make her hair look wonderful despite the Cleveland summer humidity.

Adele set down the brush and ran her hand over Katie's hair. Silently, she began braiding. She reached the end of the braid. She held it for a moment, then Katie pulled it in front of her face and held it under her wrinkled nose.

Her eyes sparkled with mischief. "Let's cut it off."

Adele gasped and sprang to her feet. "*A bob*? Katie – NO!" A giggle fluttered in her throat. "What would the captain say?"

Katie stood and rummaged through the drawer, finally locating a pair of sewing scissors. She held them up, victoriously. "John loves me, not my hair." She held the braid and faced the mirror. "Imagine what I'll look like in a hat."

Adele wore a look of contemplation. Then she took the scissors from Katie. "Alright Katie – I will let you draw me into your plan – on one condition."

"What's that?"

"That you will cut mine!"

## ~ *Fifty-Two* ~

EXHAUSTED FROM HIS trying day in the office, John quietly unlocked the front door. He had managed to choke down a sandwich at lunch, but the stress of the afternoon had left him with no appetite.

Somehow, working on land, at the shipyard, drained him of far more energy than being out on the water. Standing at the helm, in control of the ship's wheel, he breathed in the spray of the sea wild and vast beyond. It was exhilarating.

He removed his coat and hat, placing them on the newel post at the base of the staircase and took a step up. Music wafted from the living room.

Didn't Katie know how late it was? And that he was leaving in the morning on a Great Lakes excursion? Perhaps she needed to be reminded of the time and that she should have retired by now. He understood that she was alone a good portion of the day; that she most likely didn't realize the hour.

He backed down the stairs and walked toward the music coming from the phonograph. It was a song he hadn't heard before. It held a rhythm he was unfamiliar with, but it captured his attention and drew him closer. John inhaled as he reached the pocket door, half open. He could see that the electric lights were out and that the shadows on the polished floors in front of him reflected with the magic of candlelight.

Katie obviously had no idea that he had returned home. She had her back to the doorway, dancing to the melody of the disc playing on the phonograph he had given her for her birthday; not out of the ordinary. But what stopped him in his tracks was the distinctly uninhibited hip action she added to her performance.

John scratched at the stubble on his chin. He removed his hand from the door, took a step back and stared at Katie like he'd never seen a woman before.

What had she done to her hair? John studied her.

He resisted the rather insistent primal urge to strip naked and jump her. Instead, he waited to see what else she had in store, knowing that she would be mortified if she had an inkling that she was being watched. She was abandoned, but in such an innocent way. Eventually, he knew he had to say something; something without startling her.

But before he settled on the way to announce his presence, the music ended, leaving only the popping and crackling at the end of the recording. Katie turned around with a little grin so seductive, so knowing.

She had known he was there the whole time. Watching the show.

Katie caught her breath as John crossed the short distance between them, his grin causing a blush tingeing her cheeks. He changed the disk on the phonograph, gave it a few extra cranks, then he placed the needle at the beginning of the record.

She dropped her hands from where she had been fussing with her hair.

His right cheek dimpled, like it always did when he tried not to smile. John grabbed Katie's hand and twirled her smoothly into a spin, then reeled her up against him, back to front; then back out again to the music. "Your hair … it's different." His smile didn't shift, but the seductive twinkle in his eyes turned decidedly more erotic when her hips bumped his.

"It's a bob."

He brought her into a turn and held her in a gentle embrace as the tempo of the music changed. Katie followed john's lead in a foxtrot.

John slid his hand beneath the cropped hair at the base of her neck, tilting her head back.

He smiled. "It brings out your eyes. Do you like it?"

"I feel emancipated." Katie's lips were softly parted for the taking.

"Do you want me as much as I want you?"

Katie tipped her head down, just a fraction, in a nod of assent.

## ~ Fifty-Three ~

THE SETTING SUNLIGHT was pink against his eyelids. A soft breeze blew across the early evening sky, like fingers stroking the trees along the ridge.

Little wisps of auburn hair fanned the blanket as Katie shifted her head to the side. She snorted a laugh, then slapped her hand across her mouth to silence herself.

John's eyes popped open and he smiled over at her. He reached out to squeeze her shoulder. "What's so funny?"

Katie lifted herself up onto one elbow, better to face him. She brushed a curl aside. "You are."

"Me?"

"Your face was all twitchy as you were sleeping."

"I was dreaming about a beautiful woman, with bobbed hair." he shot back, grinning that Cheshire grin again.

Katie raised a brow.

"You, my dear." John laughed.

She rolled her eyes but she couldn't seem to control the upward twitch at the corners of her lips.

John turned over onto his stomach and opened his journal. He looked out across the lake, wondering how he might describe the beautiful sunset in writing. "The sun is setting with a brilliant flare of scarlet, gold and azure."

She eyed him. "I've often wondered why you don't write poetry."

He dropped his pen. "Or how about … Bluish clouds streak through the pink and orange sky?" He sat straight up and continued with an increasing element of drama in his voice. "The sun is setting in a prism of color?"

Katie laughed, tipping her head to look at him.

John's heart swelled in his chest seeing her so happy. He threw down the journal and flipped her over on her back. "Do you remember the first night we made love?"

Katie narrowed her eyes and smiled. Memories of that night made her catch her breath. "I have relived it every night since then." A single look at his smoldering eyes told her that he was remembering too.

He caressed her shoulder, warm with affection and he spoke softly. "I have four weeks before my next trip. I want to spend every minute together."

"What on earth will we do?" she asked.

He jumped up. "We can travel, or anything you would like. The sky's the limit!"

His enthusiasm spread into Katie's veins. "Let's begin now! What shall we do first?"

He smiled, but the mischievous glint in his eyes held a quiet knowledge. The suggestion was met with no resistance from Katie.

## ~ Fifty-Four ~

Sunset turned to twilight.

They were entering the home stretch of their month-long holiday. There had been no schedules that they had followed, except for candlelight dinners and lazy breakfasts.

They had one last destination, by Katie's request; the final stop – Chicago, Illinois.

John gave Katie the grand tour of where he and Will had grown up. Main Street at dusk, the farmhouse he and Will were born. But Katie halted when her eyes centered on the barn. She picked up her pace, changing to a trot, as she continued in its direction.

"It's used primarily for storage now," John told her as he fell into step behind her. He unbolted the latch and slid the door open.

The early evening light streamed in through the doorway, bringing a sense of wonder to the scene. Katie's eyes widened.

John moved a boulder from the foundation to the door and used it as a doorstop. "We have been leasing the property to the apple orchard down the road for years now."

Katie inhaled. "It's wonderful, John."

She ran her hand along the crumbling workbench, brushing off the dirt and dust of time. She studied the names that had been carved into its surface by the two young brothers she had grown to love.

"I wish I could have known your father and your mother, John," she said with a note of sadness in her voice, as she traced the letters in John's name with her finger.

He stole a quick look at her. In the fading light, her features seemed more fragile than he'd remembered seeing them. He pulled her tight against him. The crinkles around his eyes softened as he whispered in her ear. "They both would have loved you like a daughter."

Dusk gave way to dark. As they wandered back to the car, John continued steering the conversation, revealing the plans for where they would be having dinner and spending the night.

Darkness gave way to moonrise. The glow of the streetlights reflected on the brick and concrete streets of Chicago as they arrived at the hotel.

If two empty dinner plates, a spent bottle of champagne on the room service tray and a *Do Not Disturb* sign hanging outside the door of their suite in the morning was any indication, the captain and his wife had indeed enjoyed their final evening in Chicago.

Katie awoke to sunlight. She opened her eyes, snuggled up, tight against John and sighed. His pupils adjusted as he stared out the window. He inhaled and turned to face her. He smiled.

John stroked Katie's hair. It felt like corn silk and smelled like fresh rain. "I will never understand why …" he paused, and then continued. "… when you could have chosen anywhere in the world to go …" He trailed kisses down her neck, causing her to giggle, then he went on. "… that you chose this place."

Katie climbed out of bed and walked to the window. She turned back to face John, who had already joined her, clasping his hands around her waist. "That's because Chicago gave me you."

## ~ Fifty-Five ~

*July, 1925*

JOHN TURNED TO FACE the window so his own shadow didn't block his view. He held his breath as he studied the object in his hand. When he moved the pendant in the sunlight, he watched as the deep blue sapphires sparkled with memories.

"It's just as you asked – diamonds, sapphires and --" The man grinned as he struggled with the words, "*lake pearls.*"

John's eyes crinkled at the edges as he ran his finger, tracing the outer rim of the gold filigree. Among the four sizable sapphires adorning the perimeter of the necklace, were ten perfect diamonds, alternating with ten tiny gems, skillfully fashioned from Katie's *lake pearls.*

"Turn it over." The jeweler said, beaming.

Gently turning it over, being careful not to drop it, John smiled as he made out the engraved words on the back of the piece:


MY COMPASS ROSE

With a sigh, Katie turned her eyes to the sky, where the stars were crowded together so densely, they almost blotted out the darkness. She sighed. "I feel you John ... We must be looking at the same stars tonight." She backed away from the telescope and stared out the window. She whispered, "I love you."

There was nothing but ocean in every direction. No ships, no shore. Every inch of John's vision through the ship's telescope was filled with thousands of tiny pinpricks of light. He ran his thumb over the compass in his pocket.

A whisper floated across his heart:

*I love you.*

He smiled.

## ~ Fifty-Six ~

AUGUST HAD ROLLED IN, bringing with it the searing, moist breath of a fire-breathing dragon.

Katie knew she had other things to do; it was her market day, and she loved the market; its people, the diversity. But she felt herself being drawn to the shore. There was a restlessness she couldn't explain.

Instead, when she left the house, she ambled, following the curve on Edgecliff. And she found herself there. She stood and breathed in the lake breeze. Wind swept up the jagged cliff and slapped her backside.

Katie walked on the beach - their beach. It had been there for the nearly thirteen years she and John had lived there, just twenty-eight steps below their patch of land; their home.

She didn't know how long she stayed out there. But by the time she found herself on the back porch, daylight had slipped into the dusky part of the day.

The August air felt like an oven, prickling across her skin. Katie's head felt light from the fever again. She dabbed her forehead with the hankie from her pocket. Her head swam a little more and she steadied herself on the doorframe. Stepping back outside, in search of fresh air, she reached out for the porch railing. Suddenly everything around her went dark.

Hearing the sound of a gasp coming from the back yard, Adele glanced over her shoulder and saw Katie leaning against the doorjamb, her eyes closed. Adele raced against time, to prevent her from tumbling down the stairs.

The next thing Katie knew she was lying at the foot of the steps in the grass with Adele standing over her, saying her name over and over again.

"Katie ... **Kathleen!**"

Katie's head screeched with pain. She closed her eyes and listened to her own breathing for a few moments.

Adele knelt over her with an expression of distress. Jacques, who had heard Adele's screams from two doors down, rushed to the Stockton's back yard.

"Katie, can you hear me?" Adele pleaded.

A whistling noise rose in Katie's ears.

Jacques joined Adele, at Katie's side.

"Jacques, we've got to get her inside the house and call the doctor."

Jacques calmly smiled down at Katie as her eyes fluttered open slightly. He reached out to her and asked, "Katie – It's Jacques. I want you to hold on tightly to my neck."

Wiping away a thin layer of perspiration from her forehead, she hesitated, and then shakily put her arms around Jacques' neck.

"That's our girl. Hold on." He lifted her limp body, straightened and moved carefully up the porch steps.

✦ ✦ ✦ ✦ ✦ ✦ ✦ ✦ ✦ ✦

Adele found Katie working, as if nothing had happened, in her garden the following day. While she seemed to have rallied, Adele's concern grew. Defying Katie's protests, she insisted on assisting her in the garden.

She had gone to the kitchen to fill a pitcher with water for them. The warm air whipping through the window, sweet with honeysuckle drew Adele's attention to the sight of Katie, just beyond the porch. She did not look good.

Noting a steady stream of sweat appearing along Katie's jawline, Adele touched her arm. "Katie, may I call a doctor for you?"

Katie blotted her face and went back to pruning. "Maybe later. I am fine, really I am." She patted Adele's hand.

The following night, Katie told Adele she was going to the attic to the telescope – it always gave her such comfort to feel John with her. Adele mentioned to Jacques she was worried and asked him to check on Katie after awhile.

Jacques climbed the stairs to the attic and saw Katie at the telescope. She straightened up and began to sway; unaware anyone was in the room. Sweat glistened on her brow and plastered her blouse to her skin. Katie's eyes fluttered around the room, then settled on the window as if in gradual recognition. Quietly, she stared out into the night and counted stars. She smiled.

He took a step toward her just as her knees gave away. The attic door slammed as he hurried to Katie's side. She collapsed.

Adele met them, racing up the circular drive, her heart thumping, trying to escape from her ribcage. "I knew something was wrong." She opened the door to the kitchen and cleared the way for Jacques to take Katie to her upstairs bedroom.

Pulling back the quilt, Adele wished she could cry, but it wasn't that kind of pain. She felt numb. Jacques placed Katie in the bed. Her eyes drifted closed and she slipped into a restless sleep.

Adele sought help from Dr. Tripp, one of the doctors Katie had spoken fondly of. Allen Tripp couldn't imagine Katie Stockton - such a young, vibrant, energetic woman lying so close to death. But it was true.

Very quickly, her condition became grave. That night Katie sat up straight in her bed, dragging in a gasp so violent, it stung her throat. Then she collapsed back into her pillow as Adele ran to her side.

The next morning Adele drew in a ragged breath as she left Katie's room for a few minutes. She passed the doctor in the hallway.

He touched Adele's sleeve. "I'm afraid Katie is experiencing the worst of the illness. Captain Stockton needs to be here. Does he know she is ill? Where can he be reached?"

Through tear-filled eyes, Adele said, "He is on his return from a European voyage."

"Well, I suppose he will be here as soon as could be physically possible," he sighed.

"He never dawdles – he come straight home to Katie, the minute he steps off that boat." She met Dr. Tripp's eyes. "What can I do to help?"

"All we can do now is keep her comfortable, hydrated and keep watch for any symptoms; Malaise, fever, stomach pain."

Throughout that night and most of the next two days, Adele sat with Katie.

Jacques appeared in the doorway. He had fresh stems with new buds from Katie's wild rose garden in his hands. He ordered his wife from the room. "You need some fresh air."

Adele rose from Katie's bedside and joined him in the doorway. "She's taken a turn for the worse, and I'm so afraid we won't get word to Captain Stockton in time." She wrung her hands.

A feeble voice called to her from the bed. "Delly .. Please ... I don't want John to worry about me." Katie's eyes were sunken as she struggled to sit upright, then gave up. Adele rushed back to her and held both of her hands in her own as she sat back down in the chair.

Katie smiled at Adele weakly. "I need you to be strong; for me and for John." Adele's eyes filled as Katie continued. "He can't be here – it would be an impossible task and he mustn't ever feel anything but love for me. No pain; no guilt - only happy memories."

"The captain loves you so, Katie – you are his forever rose."

Katie's eyes lit up slightly with gratitude, but she replied, "I'm afraid the bloom is off the rose."

Adele sighed and smiled back through blurry eyes. "Never."

"I need you to tell John how much I love him ... I will forever, and that I will always be with him. Help him see how happy he's made me. I was an empty vessel before John." Her eyes fluttered closed, causing Adele to place her head against her chest to be sure she was still breathing.

Katie took a few rattling breaths, then came awake with a start and whispered, "Mama ..." Then she relaxed and smiled.

Adele closed her eyes. Her fingernails dug into the palms of her hands. Jacques turned his head to the window and wiped his cheek with his rolled-up shirtsleeve.

## ~ Fifty-Seven ~

*THE COMPASS ROSE* plowed through the waves, driving toward her destination back home. John impatiently watched as they moved from lock to lock, holding himself back from jumping out with a bucket, to speed up the process. He laughed at the thought.

He trained his telescopic sight on the horizon, as the city of Cleveland came into view. He registered the information in the ship's logbook. Then his own journal beckoned him, and he opened its cover.

When she docked, it took every bit of self-restraint to keep him from leaping overboard, instead of waiting for the gangplank to lower.

John hurriedly disembarked with what appeared to be a watch chain dangling from his hand. He was elated.

The taxi dropped him off in front of the driveway. Captain Stockton strolled briskly up the walk, toward the house. He was happy to be home - to see Katie again, and to give her the necklace.

John had come to an important revelation – a decision that would change his life. And Katie's.

He grinned as he imagined the look on his wife's face as he told her this had been his last voyage; he couldn't wait to tell her that he would be taking a less active interest in the traveling part of the business. He wanted to spend the rest of his life in Cleveland, to be near Katie all the time.

Fog rose in an eerie mist, weaving between the rose bushes as he approached the house.

John became aware of a lone candle in the picture window - he was overcome with a sense of sadness and fear. Desperation washed over him and he lunged for the doorknob, but it opened before he could grasp the handle.

Jacques was at the door, Adele standing beside him. Cold dread pierced John's heart. As the door closed behind him, there was silence. Then, from outside, all that could be heard was the sound of shattering glass.

## ~ *Fifty-Eight* ~

*October, 1925*

THE SOUND OF a key in the front lock brought his attention to the door as Will let himself in.

"It's a fine evening, John. Come along with me for a ride in the new coupe. It will do you good to be out. You haven't been out for two weeks; not since ..." He choked on the words.

"... since we went to the cemetery to see Katie's marker?" His shoulders went taut. "Will, is it that difficult for you to say?"

"I didn't want to start you thinking again."

John closed his journal and stood, stretched and wandered over to the window. "I truly appreciate Jacques bringing you to Cleveland, and I have enjoyed your company over the past weeks, Will, but I believe it's time you moved on, back to your own life."

Will opened the front door and pointed at his brother. He tossed John's coat at him. Without thinking, the captain's hand reached up in the air, and he caught it just before it hit the floor.

John said, "I will go for a ride with you. But only if I may drive."

The backdrop of noise from traffic in the streets created a buffer around them as John positioned himself in the driver's seat and slammed the door. He faced Will with a smile and backed out on to the street. The lampposts that lined the streets lighted the way like diamonds.

Will was concerned at the speed John was driving. He held tight onto the edges of his seat, teeth tightly clenched. "Aren't you going a little fast?" he asked John.

John rapidly changed lanes and tailgated the car in front of them. He gave the horn a toot. "Bah! This is no more than a leisurely pace, Will." Behind them, lights and buildings flashed past.

Will's knuckles began to show some sign of color again as John made the turn onto Edgecliff.

"We were only going the speed limit."

Will whistled. "It sure felt like you were going faster than that."

Once they were idling, back in the driveway, Will spoke again. "John, you are more important to me than anyone – or anything. I want to stay as long as you need me."

"I don't wish to be coddled – I am quite well."

Will studied his brother for a few minutes, beginning to believe he might be right. "I will agree to go back home as long as you give me your word that you are well enough now, and that I will hear from you on a regular basis."

Once they were back inside the house, John patted Will on the back and smiled. "Of course; I will write, wire and perhaps even a telephone call or two." He removed a bottle from the liquor cabinet and set it out on the top, with two glasses. Ironically, although it had remained illegal since the dawn of the decade, alcohol was never in short supply. "And, I assure you, Will – I am more than satisfactory – I am fine."

The captain was also a very good actor.

* * * * * * * * * * * * *

John found it hard to believe the sun still came up and the breeze still floated puffball clouds across the Cleveland sky. The wind whistled in his ear and rustled through the scrub along the Erie shoreline, competing with the roar of the lake as he resumed his morning walks.

The heat of summer was gone, leaving days of blue skies and a strong breeze off the lake, carrying the scent of the approaching winter.

Then one day, John went to the office, something he hadn't done since Katie's death. His secretary, Ann, jumped up from behind her desk to greet him with a smile.

"Captain Stockton – It's so good to have you back. We've missed you!"

But John walked right past her, and disappeared into his office. He closed the door behind him. He was quiet for a moment, then he walked up to the glass and leaned his head against it.

She immediately made a telephone call to his assistant. "Ernest, it's Ann. Can you stop by? I am worried about Captain Stockton. Yes, he's here, but he walked right past me like I was a ghost – I don't think he even saw me." She hung up the receiver when she heard the office door open again.

John pressed his hands against the frosted glass panel on his door and spoke, "Ann, have I done a good job of running this company?"

"Don't be silly. Captain, you have done a wonderful job."

"Maybe too good." He ran his hand along one of the bookcases under the window. "Maybe if I hadn't done such a damn good job of running the business, I wouldn't have been such a miserable failure as a husband to Katie – and I would have been able to save her. It's my fault she had to die alone." He swallowed the lump in his throat.

Ann touched John's arm. "Nobody could have saved her. She was ill, captain. The doctors couldn't save her; you certainly couldn't have."

He retreated into his office. Ann followed him. "Captain, you are being too hard on yourself. There was never a more devoted husband. How can we make you see how happy Katie was? Why, she lit up at the very sound of your name." She smiled wistfully.

His eyes darkened. "Damn it all, woman! I should have stayed with her, instead of roaming the Great Lakes and traipsing the world!" He carefully lowered himself into his chair just as Ernest Kennedy appeared in the doorway.

Ernest looked over his shoulder to the door and said, "I need to talk to the captain alone." Ann patted John's arm and left the two alone in the office.

John stood and looked out the window at the boats, strung like beads along the harbor. "So, how's the business doing? He clasped his hands behind his back and stared out.

"It would be far better if you were here, sir."

John's eyebrows rose. He faced his assistant. "What makes you say that, Kennedy?" he asked pragmatically.

Ernest took an instinctive step forward. He hesitated. "John, we need your leadership."

John muttered a few choice words then turned his attention back to the window. "From what I see by the books, we are doing quite well under your fine leadership." He stepped back and walked to the door.

They traded glances.

"I don't know when I will be ready to return to the office. In the meantime, Ernest, I want you to take complete charge of operations in my absence."

Kennedy blinked, his eyes huge and owl-like behind his glasses. "What? John ..." he wiped the beads of sweat from his forehead with his handkerchief and quickly returned it to his pocket.

"You've been doing the job for months already. The only difference will be that now you'll be getting paid for it." John grinned as he exited past Ann, who was just outside the door. "Ann! Were you eavesdropping again?"

He winked, but she could see the sadness in his eyes.

Friends were growing increasingly more concerned about John Stockton and his state of mind. What was Katie's death doing to the captain? Would it send him into a downward spiral of dark despair?

Nobody had seen him in days, when Jacques got the notion to use the house key he had been given months before.

It was almost noon. Jacques knocked on the door to John's bedroom. When there was no response, he quietly turned the doorknob.

John's face was buried in the pillow. He slowly lifted his head, his hair disheveled, with four days growth of beard, looking like a vagabond. His clothes, the same he had worn the day before, were all crumpled and creased.

"Captain, I brought you some food." Jacques said as he approached his bedside with a tray of buttered toast and fruit. "You must keep up your strength."

Without a word, Captain Stockton swung his legs over the edge of the bed and planted his bare feet on the cold floor. Jacques waited until he saw him take a bite of toast, and he slowly backed out of the room. "Adele will come by later."

John spent the afternoon slumped in a leather armchair facing the window, staring out at the lake.

## ~ Fifty-Nine ~

THE CAPTAIN'S DESPONDENCY grew by the day. The weeks slowly passed into months. The greatness of his loss began to overwhelm him.

John's fingers stiffened on the dials of his telescope sight as he studied the ships coming toward the harbor.

With his heart in his throat, he pulled a cloth bag from his pocket and dumped its contents into his open palm. Katie's pendant stared back at him. John buried his face in his hands, his whole body tingling with sadness. He closed his eyes tightly, as if not allowing pain to enter.

John had been in the attic for two days, looking through old photographs and the telescope, choosing to remain up there, sleeping in his bedroom back at the house and eating little of the trays Jacques and Adele had brought up to him.

After John had assured them that he was fine, Jacques and Adele accepted an invitation to an art show over the long weekend.

"Captain, are you positive you will be alright?" Adele said as John walked them to the front door.

He nodded. "Of course. Go now. Enjoy your holiday." He stretched his lips to an unconvincing smile. Then the captain locked the doors of his life and withdrew from the world.

He stopped outside the carriage house. He pressed his hand to the doorjamb and he gazed up at the window - to the same spot he and Katie had spent many nights together.

He had no idea how long he'd been there, but the sound of the driving rain summoned him back to the house. John flicked the switch by the living room doorway and the light came on. Just then, lightning flashed in the window. The light went out.

Lucas Camden's final words to him came flowing back to John as he turned to retreat from the room. "The world is hastily evolving, son. But never forget … No incandescent electric bulb will ever compete with the warmth and beauty of candle flame."

The light in his eyes changed. His gloom flared into angry fire. Captain Stockton reached out and grabbed the cobalt blue lamp from the table, ripping the cord from its socket. He smashed it against the fireplace, missing the window by a fraction of an inch.

Then quite calmly, as if nothing had happened, he picked up his journal from the table, carried it to the chair and he took a seat. He smoothed the page of the journal, wrote the day's date at the top, and began his entry.

John wrote about Katie – about the compass rose pendant. It evoked a smile from him – until he realized he didn't have the necklace with him.

*The compass rose!* He searched in a wild panic through all of the rooms in the house, but there was no sign of it. He found himself back in front of the picture window.

Where was it? John couldn't remember when he last looked at it. "It must be in here somewhere," he breathed, his eyes scanning the brimming shelves.

He caught a glimpse of something sparkling from across the parlor. An object was sitting on the ledge of the picture window. John raced over to the window seat, only to find a brass ring from the lamp he had just destroyed. His chest tightened. He dropped to the floor and laid his head on the blue seat cushion – where he fell asleep.

The following morning, John woke with a start, his eyes struggling to adjust to the sunlight beating down on him through the window.

So much for everything looking better in the morning.

He needed to get up, to begin a new day, but the mere sound of his groan hurt John's already throbbing head.

He rose as the recollection of the previous night returned to him. There was broken glass scattered over the floor. In the morning sunlight, spilling in through the window, the shards sparkled like crushed sapphires and tiny diamonds.

John was infuriated. After several hours of searching frantically, resulting in failure, he came to a decision. It was a decision that made little sense, even to him, but his mind was made up. He must do whatever it took to recover Katie's pendant.

The carpenter wiped his brow and asked again. *"You want us to do what?"*

"I said I want you to tear out the floors."

*"Sir - All of them? Are you sure this is what you want?"*

Captain Stockton whirled toward him. Anger boiled inside him like a pot on a stove. "Don't dare to question me! Yes, I will rip up every single floorboard if I have to! And I want to inspect each room as it is completed."

In the morning, the team of carpenters arrived at the house. As they walked through the foyer, each one marveled at the craftsmanship that had gone into every detail of the construction of the structure.

A small crowd had assembled out by the curb, as the last carpenter arrived.

"Isn't this the guy who had the bricks in the chimney laid so that they formed some sort of star?"

The mailman pointed to the chimney. "It's called a compass rose. He told me it was so the ships out on the lake can find their way."

"Oh, that's nonsense," another man scoffed.

A woman held her hand over her heart. "Maybe so, but I find it wonderfully romantic."

"I heard they will be dismantling the floors, plank by plank," one bystander said to another." Then he scratched his head. "…Which is interesting in itself, isn't it?"

Another man answered him, shaking his head slowly. "He's the most meticulous man I have ever known, and that just doesn't seem like something he would do."

It soon became apparent that John was looking for something – searching frantically. The crew working in the house speculated that he must have lost something.

But what could possibly be so important that he would risk destroying all of the beautiful, handcrafted hardwood floors?

The following three days were a blur for John Stockton.

Jacques and Adele returned to a disaster zone. Jacques took the staircase, three steps at a time as he bolted up to the master bedroom, searching for John. He reappeared at the top of the stairs and gripped the banister in disbelief. He slowly made his way back to the foyer, in shock.

The door handle twisted; the pocket doors parted. Light flooded in from beyond the door. A silhouette resembling Jacques Laurent appeared. He sighed heavily and stepped over the rubble at his feet.

"Captain?"

There he stood, looking like a man who'd just spent the night making love to a bottle of 20 year-old bourbon. John quickly retreated and stepped into a corner full of shadows. He stared at the blank wall.

Jacques ran his hand over his face. "What are you doing? This is madness!"

The captain looked a little dazed. "I lost Katie's compass rose pendant. I must search everywhere for it."

"How can you possibly think that you lost it in the floor?" Jacques raised his voice. Then he took him by the shoulders and his voice softened. "John – please listen to me. Even if the compass rose was in the floor and you found it … *Then what?*" Jacques tried to reason with him. "How do you intend to put everything back together; in its place?"

"Are you referring to my life?" John dropped to the chair behind the table.

"Of course, I am referring to the floors! Captain, I beg you to stop this now!" Jacques, nearly in tears picked up two splintered planks of cherry, as if he was in great pain.

After a brief moment of silence, John answered him. "Perhaps you are right. I will have the crew begin salvaging what they can, in the morning."

"Captain – may I oversee the work to restore the floors?" Jacques clutched the planks to his chest as if they were his children. "Please allow me this honor."

John slapped his hands on the table and pushed back his chair. "You are the best man for the job!" He roared with laughter, and took a step toward Jacques, who thought for a moment he was going to hug him.

~ *Sixty* ~

DID YOU TELEPHONE WILLIAM?" Adele shifted the baby from one hip to the other.

Jacques peeked out from behind the easel. "Yes. He will return as soon as he can arrange to have someone take over his job while he is here. It could be another month."

"Do you think he will be able to help the captain?"

"He is planning to join John in the business. This is something that John has wanted for a long time. We are hoping that this will be what he needs to move along with his life."

"What about his own life, in Ireland?"

"He will keep everything as it is. Once the captain is strong enough, Will may return to Ireland."

"Captain, I have an idea." Jacques stood as the carpenter continued pegging cherry planks at the threshold leading from the living room into the foyer. He picked up a chunk of milled black walnut and held it against a piece of cherry and one of maple with a split running along its side. "We have many of these damaged planks. They don't match anything."

"And your point?" John looked at him inquisitively.

Jacques gathered the odd pieces, of various dimensions and species and began laying them across the newly completed floor in the living room. He straightened and glanced up at the captain. "How do you feel about inlay designs?"

The captain tilted his head to one side. "What did you have in mind?"

Jacques proceeded to lay the various pieces of wood, forming a rough pattern that began to take the shape of a slightly crude star. Then he unfolded a paper he had in his pants pocket and handed it to John.

John turned the paper around and studied it from all angles. Then he folded it back up and handed it back to Jacques, with no expression.

Jacques was confused by the captain's silence and absence of emotion. However, he wasn't surprised. He had gotten used to the unpredictable quirkiness that had come to define John Stockton since Katie's death. He waited and he watched as a wry grin creeped across the captain's face.

"A compass rose! Excellent idea - Start on it in the morning!"

The carpenter, who had been listening to the conversation, shook his head as he walked out the door. He wiped his hands on his overalls. "Are you sure? It just doesn't seem like common sense to me, sir."

John spun back around and glared at him. *"Common sense?"* He gestured wildly with his open hand in the air. "Who said anything about common sense?"

John ascended the stairs and paused at the portrait of Katie. Then he smiled and continued.

## ~ Sixty-One ~

PUSHING ASIDE HIS THOUGHTS, Jacques inspected the inlaid strips of wood that had been set into the floor, studying the design from different angles.

John stopped near the bottom of the staircase and stared back up at the portrait of Katie. And he didn't move for at least fifteen minutes.

John called Jacques into his office. "Come with me."

Once he had joined him, John sat and motioned for Jacques to sit across from him. "Now, I am the one with the idea, Jacques."

Jacques sat back in the chair as John began his dialogue. "You are a painter by trade, are you not?"

"I am an artist, sir."

"Whatever you call it, you are a painter, no?"

Jacques shrugged. "Yes."

"I'd like to see Katie wearing the compass rose pendant."

Jacques broke into a sweat, wondering if the man was crazy enough to suggest Katie's grave be dug up, just so he could see the necklace around her neck." His brain refused to process the rest of that thought.

No, that couldn't possibly have been what the captain had in mind. Jacques' expression changed from worry to relief with John's next words. "I want you to paint the compass rose into the portrait."

"But captain – this is such a beautiful work of art. The passion I feel from this painting could start a fire. I wouldn't dare to alter it."

"Very well, Jacques. I shall find another artist to do it for me."

The sound of Jacques' heart breaking could be heard throughout the house. He followed the captain into the hall. "Captain."

Stockton turned to face him.

"Adele and I loved her as well. It would be my honor to paint the pendant into Katie's portrait."

$$\star_\star\star\star\;\star_\star\star\;\star\;\star\;\star\;\star\;\star\;\star_\star\star$$

Jacques' fingers were trembling as he removed the finished painting from the easel.

He studied it later, leaning against the wall, ready to be hung. He was pleased. He climbed the ladder and placed the picture back in its original location. He descended the stairs to view his work. He grinned as he noticed Adele and their baby in the foyer.

When Adele saw the portrait hanging on the wall, she suddenly became quiet and then tilted her head slightly downward.

"What is it, Adele? Should I have done something different?"

Adele shook her head and raised her chin. "No, Jacques, it's beautiful - the floor *and* the portrait. Jacques - I am worried about the captain." She sat the baby on the floor and began wringing her hands, nervously. "Why, just look at all the things he's been doing these past few months. You must have witnessed his abnormal behavior, too."

Jacques and Adele entered the living room and paused as they observed Stockton at the picture window. Oblivious that they were even in the room, the captain walked to the fireplace and stood staring into the cold ashes where there had once been firelight.

Then he turned back and faced the window again. His eyes were calm yet unreadable as he gazed out at the view of the lake.

Suddenly, he looked back at them wildly, and then put his face in his hands. His body shook with the force of his effort to control his emotions.

Adele jumped. Jacques took her elbow and they turned to leave the room. She picked up the baby and headed for the door. But the captain called Jacques back. "Jacques, Join me in my office."

By the time Jacques arrived in the office, John was sitting at his desk, rifling through his desk drawer, tossing aside rubber bands, pins and shreds of paper. With a triumphant grin, Captain Stockton pulled out an envelope and handed it to Jacques. He laughed ruefully and slammed the desk drawer closed.

John exhaled and peered at Jacques through his spectacles, his eyes distorted slightly by the glass. Jacques folded back the envelope flap and opened it slowly. Inside, staring up at him was a document. His name was at the top.

"But captain – this has my name on it."

"A remarkable coincidence, wouldn't you say?" He drummed his fingers on the desktop.

Jacques' eyes dropped to the middle of the page. It was the deed to the cottage. The document had been notarized and across the middle were the stamped words: PAID IN FULL.

Jacques was dumfounded. Numb with disbelief, hands shaking, he said, "Sir, I cannot accept this – you are too generous."

The captain removed his spectacles. He wiped the glass lenses on a corner of his jacket and then put them back on, carefully wrapping the wires behind each ear. He laughed sadly and ran his fingers through his hair. "Nonsense."

Then, with a wave of his hand, he dismissed Jacques and walked to the door.

He turned back and said, "Besides - it's too late – your name is already on the deed. The house belongs to you."

~ *Sixty-Two* ~

WILL RETURNED TO CLEVELAND at the end of the month, the logic behind the move being that maybe, if he joined John in the shipping business, it would draw him out of the depression that had engulfed him.

At first, they were both happy with that decision. John enjoyed having his brother alongside him in the office. But it soon became evident that being confined to an office was not William's cup of tea.

Will stood at the office window, watching as cargo was being moved from the dock to a freighter, when John entered the room.

"That's a lot of cargo." Will said.

"Loads of it. Oil, grains, scrap metal, tobacco and mail - Canada needs it all." John sat down, pushed his chair away from his desk and crossed his ankle over his knee.

William began thinking about reviving the *Compass Rose* – it hadn't made a voyage since the one John returned from, finding Katie gone. It just might be the thing to bring John back to life again. At first, when he brought up the subject, the captain slid his chair up to the desk and ignored him.

Will stuck his hands in his pockets and stared back at him. "John, she's a great vessel, in top condition."

Captain Stockton looked up over the glow of his banker's lamp and raised a brow.

Will went on. "I want to sail on the *Compass Rose.*"

Gritting his teeth, John lifted his eyes to meet his brother's. His throat tightened and he swallowed. "She's not going out – hasn't been out in more than a year. I don't even know where most of the crew is." He picked up a framed photograph from the desk. Will took it from him and studied the faded image of the boat, taken just after she returned from her maiden voyage, years ago.

Will continued, "With you, captain."

Easing himself back onto the chair, John laced his fingers together. "Why the sudden interest?"

"I think it's about time I got to experience for myself, firsthand, the lure of the water that has hypnotized my dear brother for so many years. Perhaps I have missed my own calling."

John smiled a smile that was almost his old self. He had to concede that this might be true. He stood. His eyes softened. "Well said."

# ~ Sixty-Three ~

*September, 1926*

HE WALKED ALONG the dock toward the *Compass Rose* with John. The sea bag given to him by his big brother made Will feel a little like he was heading off to school again.

The ship was even more beautiful up close. The feeling of power and endurance was almost overwhelming. The crane grumbled as it lowered a section of cargo into position, the men guiding it with ropes.

September had dawned in Cleveland, and it was sweltering. The heat poured down and John's shirt was wet. He lit a cigarette and swallowed hard, as he fought an incredible force, pulling him toward the *Compass Rose.* He made his way slowly up the gangway with Will and looked up at the bridge where he spotted Captain Hale.

John had declined the invitation to sail with the crew. Too many memories fought their way into his head. No, it would not have been a wise decision.

Just a hair over six feet tall, Thomas Hale was a bit on the stocky side, and wore a dark, neatly trimmed beard. Hale had been in a serious accident three years back. It had claimed the index finger from his left hand, but it never interfered with his capabilities. Hale led Will down a narrow stairwell to the deck below, where he pointed to a small closet. "You can join us after you store your bag in there."

Then, returning to the bridge, Captain Hale turned to John. "Captain – I would gladly relinquish my duties, if you'd reconsider accompanying us. It would truly be my honor, sir." He walked toward the wheelhouse.

Without a word, John made his way slowly to the tiny room filled with time-honored, exquisite textures of wood and brass. Thomas observed as John took hold of the wheel. His eyes lit up. He smiled.

He studied the grain of the wood, bringing to mind the day the new wheel was fitted to the mechanism at the helm. The energy he felt by touching it, transported him to another place; another time.

John had taken such pride and joy that he had been able to keep the spirit of that old tree alive in so many distinctive ways, fourteen years ago. His mind wandered for a moment, recalling the doors that had been hand crafted from the old oak.

He felt the timeless rhythm of the open sea as he held tight to the wheel. Captain John Stockton owned three-quarters of the world when he was at the wheel of the *Compass Rose*.

His grip slid slightly, but he regained his grasp, allowing the lake breeze to sweep against his face and the captain abruptly returned to the present.

John breathed in through his nose and puffed back out. So few men would ever have the opportunity to hold the world in their hands … to speak to seabirds as they dance to the melody of the water.

But his hands began to shake on the wheel as reality sank in. Too much had happened. It was too soon for him to return to the *Compass Rose* – perhaps the time would never come again.

"The tugboats are in place and ready to escort us out of the harbor, sir."

John backed away from the wheel. He set his jaw and opened his eyes. "No." Heat burst into his cheeks as he faced the gangplank. "I can't." He extended his hand to Captain Hale, who nodded at John's firm handshake.

John turned to his brother and slapped him on the back. "It will be difficult for me to wait to hear of your adventure, Will." He offered the crew a weak smile and a salute. Then Captain Stockton hastily disembarked.

Amid two blasts of the ship's horn, the crew took their respective places. Will ran one hand along the rail as he walked, observing the gangplank being hauled up. He watched the crew, positioned at the bow and the stern, unwinding thick ropes from the capstans on the dock.

John's thoughts carried him to another time. Being on the fantail of the *Compass Rose*, lined up with his crew for the christening ceremony, John Stockton had never felt taller. It seemed so long ago to him now.

An odd feeling overcame John; a combination of happiness for the *Compass Rose* – that she was no longer land-bound. But there was also a profound sadness; she was leaving him behind.

The *Compass Rose* eased away from the quayside and nosed her way slowly out of the harbor, with the help of two tugboats.

Captain Stockton observed as she disappeared into the horizon.

## ~ Sixty-Four ~

IN THE DISTANCE, thunder sounded, muffled and menacing. Dark clouds churned against the sky – the storm was almost on them.

The ocean parted with a long continuous shush as the *Compass Rose*, the great steamer she was, clocked in well ahead of the Atlantic storm.

The crew paid little attention to the slant of the deck and the ominous creak of the unknown that was upon them.

Eyeing the heavy rain clouds approaching, still getting his sea legs, the doorway saved Will from falling as he gripped it with his right hand. He asked, "The sky looks terribly threatening. Will we be safe?"

"We can outrun the rest of the gale, with any luck," Hale said checking the brass ship's clock with his pocket watch, just to be sure. "Only a ship this strong and well-made would stand a chance," he said, staring at the sinister clouds gathering in the sky.

Lightning zigzagged across the Atlantic, followed by a deafening clap of thunder. "We have to get - - - !" The thunder drowned out his words but there was no question what he was saying.

The crew worked tirelessly to protect the ship from what they were about to be faced with.

On the darkened deck, just after daybreak, Captain Hale clutched the lifeline with both hands as he made his way to the bridge. The ship gave a sudden lurch, sending him hurtling across the wooden boards.

"The wind is shifting - coming in from the Bahamas." Hale continued staring out at the storm. He pushed against the panic and ordered his men to stuff themselves into the main cabin. The surf was raging. He shut the door and windows to muffle it.

Something hit hard against the door. The windows shattered. Dim slivers of daylight came in around the banging doorframe as the wind chipped away at it. He latched the door for a moment and gave orders.

"If the wind gets worse, or water comes in, man the lifeboats. I will remain with her!" Hale flung open the hatch and turned to his crew. His voice shouted against the waves of sea spray and air, pelting his face. "Don't latch the doors!"

Never-ending waves continued to loom above the *Compass Rose* in the darkness. The deck heaved up and down. Her bow pierced a wave, and seawater gushed over the forward section of the deck. Will braced his feet, turned his back, and gasped as icy water sloshed over him. Rain stung his face and arms.

The *Compass Rose* hurled and thrashed, turning in circles as if looking for an escape from the hurricane. Broken boards flew across the surface and shredded metal spun, swirling in the air overhead.

The wind ripped the hatch off the deck; it flipped and tumbled in the air. By then, the water was over Captain Hale's knees and the waves were cresting over the bow, sweeping and claiming anything in their way. The rain continued in, seizing and scratching across everything in sight.

Blinded by a curtain of driving rain, Hale called from the rear through a megaphone, shouting through the wind, directing the lifeboats be put over the side and partially lowered. Even if they were able to escape in the lifeboats, the odds weren't in their favor. But remaining aboard would give them absolutely no chance for survival at all.

The storm continued to pound the *Compass Rose*, waves coming aboard, smashing in windows and doors. They huddled below, listening to the wood and metal crack; the *Compass Rose* was splintering into a thousand pieces.

The heavens released a howling fury. The storm raged on, creating several moments of false hopes that the fury of the storm might be over, only to be swept away by the wrath of the hurricane as quickly as hope had appeared on the scene.

The storm had ripped off one of the lifeboats and all of the lockers on the deck. A ladder nearly claimed Will, as it flew past him. The *Compass Rose* groaned, listing hard to port. Echoes of anguish were deadened by the sound of screeching metal.

"*Abandon ship* ..." The words strangled in Hale's throat. A sudden gust of wind tore his words to shreds. Then a deafening, rolling, thunderous roar saturated the atmosphere around them.

Suddenly something changed. The wind shifted and transformed into little wisps of air. There was an eerie calmness in the sky. The rain ceased. A thin golden halo appeared around the edges of the indigo purple cloud overhead. The sun was emerging.

One by one, the men onboard the *Compass Rose* gathered on the deck, gazing into the incandescent sky. As relief spread across their weary faces, the jubilation in their voices was unmistakable.

The rose-gold of the sun peeking out around the cloud, seemed to burnish the deck's surface, giving its stacks, masts and everything around them an uncanny radiance.

The sky looked like it had been freshly washed, the air releasing a sweet fragrance as they moved about the deck. They were suddenly very aware of the sun on their faces and the warm breeze touching their skin.

Through Will's blurred vision, he noticed that the deck remained tilted at a strange angle. He marveled at the crew of the *Compass Rose* as they began cleaning the deck of the debris. Emptying buckets of water over the side into the ocean, he found it incredible that they were still afloat.

First Mate, Paul Morgan, appeared from around the side of the cabin and approached Captain Hale. "I think you need to see this. I just saw the damage to the hull." He motioned for Hale to join him. Will followed.

Hale's expression was grim. "How bad is it?"

Morgan gestured as he turned and led him and two other crewmen across the slanting quarterdeck and down below. Hale's head throbbed as he bent over to survey the destruction.

Leaking compartments would have been an understatement, to say the least.

It wasn't possible. Five cavernous holes in the hull, under the sea level – clear through all of the walls - openings they could see right through, to the water – in five separate places. But no water was coming in – not a single drop. He wiped the sweat from his brow. Nobody spoke.

Hale held his hand, the one with the missing finger, in front of one of the gaping holes – the biggest one. Then, as he began trembling uncontrollably, Will reached past him and put his own hand completely through the cavity.

*"Ho-ly cow,"* Will breathed as he quickly drew his hand back. It was dripping with water – seawater. He looked at the ragged openings again and did a double take.

Captain Hale could find no words. There was no explanation for it. Was it too late? Were they dead?

By all rights, the *Compass Rose* should have been on her way to the bottom of the Atlantic Ocean. But she was still afloat; her entire crew safely aboard. Hale willed himself to stop trembling like a leaf in the wind.

When they found their way back to the deck, they noticed something. They were no longer slanting. Hale made a sound of disbelief. A loud one.

Was this some kind of message from heaven?

Or from hell?

## ~ Sixty-Five ~

WHEN JOHN IMAGINED the twisted, broken wreckage, he wept. It was as though the scab had just been ripped off his heart. He uttered a wordless cry of grief.

Captain Stockton received word that The *Compass Rose* was feared lost in a hurricane off the coast of Miami, Florida. There was no trace of her to be found. Anywhere.

John rose and went to the window. With one hand resting on the glass, he tried to angle his face to receive the sun's warmth.

Sparing no expense, John arranged for a round-the-clock, search-and-rescue effort beyond what the US Coast Guard already had in place, personally financing the effort and traveling to the region himself.

On the seventh day, the effort was suspended.

Captain Stockton hardly recognized his own voice, cool and remote; as untouchable as the rings around Saturn. So much had gone wrong that he was afraid to hope anymore. "What you are telling me is that she just disappeared; that those 28 lives simply no longer exist?" An invisible band wrapped around his chest and cut off his breath.

"Captain, I assure you – we have exhausted every avenue available; we just can't explain it." The lieutenant removed his cover, wiping the sweat from his brow. "You have my word that the moment we find anything – any sign of her – you will be the first to hear."

A stream of curses flew from John's mouth.

Captain Stockton returned home to Cleveland, even more distraught than before. The Friday after he returned home, John received a telephone call from Lou Phillips.

Adele knocked quietly on the door to the captain's den.

"What is it?" He responded, without turning away from the window.

"Captain – you have a telephone call."

"Who is it?"

She parted the double doors. "He says his name is Lou Phillips."

John didn't move. "I don't know any Lou Phillips." He continued staring out the window, the shadow of raindrops on his face making them look like tears.

Adele stepped back out to the table in the foyer and held the receiver and mouthpiece up to her face. After a few minutes, she returned to the den. She stopped just behind John, her hand on his shoulder. "Mr. Phillips says he is William's attorney."

John sat on the floor and rested his head on the window seat. "I have nothing to say over the telephone. If this *Mr. Phillips* wishes to speak to me, I will do so only if he meets with me and my own attorney, in person."

The meeting was arranged between Phillips, Stockton and Harold Archer for Thursday morning. Mr. Archer, a remarkable eighty-one-year-old, had represented Lucas Camden and his successor, John Stockton, after the transfer of the business, in 1907. He was gentle looking, with kind, compassionate eyes, wire-rimmed glasses and gray hair, which was thinning at the top.

Lou Phillips explained that he was the liaison between William's legal representation in Ireland and any corresponding legal affairs, in the US.

John was the only beneficiary named in William Stockton's Last Will and Testament. At the close of the official meeting, Harold Archer stayed back. "Stockton, I want to speak with you."

The captain drew a deep breath, massaging the skin between his eyes as his attorney continued. "John, I know this is not a good time, but this does bring up an important question you must address."

John picked up his journal and turned his head slightly.

"It's time you had a proper will; an iron-clad legal document on file for yourself."

The captain appeared lost in thought for a few moments. Then he faced Mr. Archer. "I want to leave everything to charity."

"*All* of your worth, John?"

John removed a book from the shelf under the window. He placed it on the corner of his desk, the exact corner, repositioning it until its edges match the edges of the wood precisely. "Yes." Then he added, "With one exception. I wish for the house to live on, in Katie's memory."

"John, you know that's just not possible. Houses need upkeep – and that costs money."

"Should anything happen to me, I will trust my friend, Jacques Laurent, to be caretaker. I shall put funds in a trust account."

"And what if Mr. Laurent cannot or does not wish to?"

"Then I would like for him to find a suitable caretaker."

"John, do you know how difficult that will be to accomplish? You can't provide funds until infinity."

"Then I want a stipulation put in there, that should the caretaker no longer be able to keep the house, it will be up to his personal discretion to sell it to someone he feels worthy of the house."

"But how …?"

"How the hell should I know?"

"John, be reasonable. I understand what you must be going through. But you can't change the past."

"You're right Harold. I *can't* change the past." A shudder ripped through him. "I can only relive it one brutal memory at a time."

"Captain …" Archer hesitated.

"No more questions - *just make it happen!*" And John stormed out of the room.

## ~ Sixty-Six ~

TWO WEEKS LATER, Archer returned to the house. He sat in a chair on the back porch and waited for John to return from his walk.

"You drive a hard bargain, captain." Archer smiled as John approached him. "My heart nearly gave out on this one."

The will was a cross between a legal document and something that resembled damn good science fiction.

"This *should* work," Harold Archer said as he handed the pen to John. "However, should it be questioned, I've built in enough complicated roadblocks, diversions and specific stipulations that would tie up the process indefinitely, it's doubtful that anybody will bother contesting it."

John didn't hesitate as he began to pen his signature.

"Don't you want to read it first, John?"

John shook his head and finished recording his *John Hancock*. "I trust you, Harold." He signed the remaining two copies and put down the pen. "I have no concerns, knowing you will be there to see this through."

Mr. Archer stiffened in the chair. "This is my last official day as a practicing attorney. I'm afraid I won't be handling the other end of this one, John."

"Archer," Stockton leaned in with an impish grin, "You're not old. You are not going anywhere."

Harold held his hand out to John. "Stockton – I've been at this for fifty-three years; sometimes one has to admit that it's time." He patted John's hand and continued. "I have been diagnosed with terminal cancer."

The captain jumped in with, "But you can't just give up, Archer."

"Oh pshaw, Stockton – I have no intention of giving up. I fully intend to *go down with the ship*." He looked stricken the moment he realized his error.

He placed his hand on top of his head as if to be searching for hair. His voice wobbled like his chin. "Oh my God, John – I cannot believe I said that! I am so sorry."

Mr. Archer stood and faced the porch steps. "That's another reason I can't practice anymore. I used to sell snow to the Eskimos ... *now* look at me."

John stood next to him and gave him a gentle pat on the arm. "I know what you meant, Harold."

Later, standing at the kitchen sink, John stared into his own face reflected back by the darkness beyond the window. Where his eyes should have been he saw hollow spheres staring back at him. When John grasped the kitchen doorknob to go outside, he stumbled over a cardboard box sitting in his path.

*I asked Adele to put all of these in the attic. How careless of her to miss this one!*

He reached for a loose flap of the box, annoyed at her negligence. Inside, smiling up at him was a large, lopsided star, consisting of thin strips of hand-split hardwood, held together with square wooden pegs.

He lifted the wooden star from its box. A sizable piece came off as he attempted to lay it on the floor next to him. He hugged the broken star against his chest. "Will, I'm sorry. I should have taken better care of this star ... and also of you."

John placed the star back in its box and carried it up the stairs. Once in the attic, he stopped at the closet door, expecting a fight to get it open. He gathered all the strength he could in his hand and yanked hard.

The door creaked open with ease, throwing John backward onto the attic floor. He laid there, staring up at the ceiling for a moment, dumbfounded. John sat up and laughed.

*Now it opens!*

He searched feverishly through everything in the attic closet for a box large enough to fit the star and padding to protect it. That piece would never have fallen off if he had taken better care of it.

He was just about to give up when he spotted the old wooden crate, hiding in the far back corner of the closet. Stooping over as he neared the corner so he didn't hit his head, John dragged the crate from the closet into the attic, next to the workbench.

Was it what he thought it was?

He was right. The carton contained pieces of scrap oak that had been left over from the special projects John had commissioned from the fallen oak in the lot when the house was under construction. There hadn't been much useable lumber leftover, but there were a few pieces that John had admired; he'd been fascinated by the unique movement of the grain.

Once the two doors and the new ship's wheel for the *Compass Rose* had been created, he couldn't bring himself to part with the rest. So the crate sat in the attic closet, forgotten for fourteen years.

The captain rummaged through the box for a piece of scrap oak to stabilize the rickety star. He spent the next three hours, toiling over the star, pegging and nailing, replacing not one, but three pieces that had split with scraps; scraps that, ironically, were almost identical in size and shape to the ones he was replacing. Finally, he secured everything with metal clips and a few strategically placed strips he fashioned from Bakelite scraps that had been sitting on the workbench.

"I guess you and I have taken our last voyage together." He brushed the loose sawdust away and placed the star, flat inside the box, pushing cotton padding around it for safekeeping. With the final flap tucked inside the carton, he slid the box into the closet. His fingers stilled. And he smiled. He didn't know why it had never occurred to him before.

His star looked a lot like a compass rose.

＊＊＊＊＊＊＊＊＊＊＊＊＊＊＊

That afternoon, after a conversation that troubled Adele, John walked quietly out the front door.

About an hour later, strolling past the driveway with Franklin, she stopped when she saw him on the front step. "You might want to take along a coat if you will be out long."

"I don't need a coat; I don't need anything," he said, sounding like he was reading from a script.

She asked him where he was going. He just mumbled something and slowly continued, without closing the door behind him.

From his erratic behavior, she suspected that he had been drinking, but didn't want to upset him, so she said nothing and watched him uproot several struggling roses from the side of the house, as he had done for the last several weeks, stuffing them into his pockets, before pulling out of the driveway.

In actuality, John had not been drinking at all. He had been stone sober since the day he realized he had lost the pendant.

He gunned the engine again, spitting gravel beneath his wheels and made the sharp turn into the cemetery as if he was being chased. As he approached the site, John hesitated and took note of his surroundings. The hair on the back of his neck stood at attention.

Well beyond the growing season in Cleveland, there was something clearly out of synch.

The rose vines he had pulled up from Katie's garden; the ones he had left on her grave each time, on every visit, had actually taken root. Not only that, but they were thriving, against overwhelming odds.

John's eyes stared solemnly at the gray stone of Katie's grave marker as a whistling wind raced between the rows of headstones. The words carved into the stone were a cold reminder of what he had lost:

KATHLEEN ROSE STOCKTON
1892 – 1925
BELOVED WIFE
SWEET IRISH ROSE

246

A sudden balmy breeze kicked up from behind, rearranging the leaves, exposing a particularly courageous patch of pink roses. John knelt, touching the delicate buds, peeking through at him.

His scalp tingled. He studied the stone again. "Katie – Is there something you want me to hear? What is it that you are trying to tell me?"

After he returned from the cemetery, Captain Stockton found himself back home, standing in the circular driveway. As he turned up his collar, he wandered along the shoreline cliffs, searching. For what, he didn't know. After a few hours, he stopped and stared out at the lake.

The long walk had done nothing to calm his spirit; if anything, his restlessness had only heightened.

In just one year, Captain John Stockton's world had exploded like a dying star. Would he have the strength to face another day?

Doubts lingered in his mind as he began pacing again; the lake edged closer and closer. By sunset, John found himself back at the dock.

The lake was a smear of pastel gray and lavender. A breeze greeted him as he approached the water. White breakers bashed themselves against the rocky outcropping at the base of the cliff, spraying lake mist. Every now and again, he felt a sprinkle of spindrift on his face.

Through half-closed lids, he caught sight of his rowboat. It nodded in the wake at him, as if it was beckoning him to come aboard. John knew there wasn't much gas in the reserve outboard tank, but he didn't give it much thought, since the oars were laying on the floor.

The water ... that's what he needed. It was his answer to everything.

# ~ Sixty-Seven ~

SOMEHOW, THE MAGNIFICENCE of the water cleansed him.
John felt a burst of freedom as he pushed the boat away from the dock.

Like the waves rolling beneath the craft, he kept going over and
over what he should have done different. He allowed his mind to drift
back to the day they first met. He was thirty-two, she only eighteen –
young and exquisite, with a reckless spirit that had both enthralled and
terrified him. Katie had been everything he wanted in a companion –
strong and determined, yet gentle and loving.

And she stirred his soul for thirteen years.

How could he go on without her?

John felt a coldness in the pit of his stomach. He stared down at
the water, a strange radiance from the moon surrounding the boat,
dancing a subtle glittery dance.

Katie's face softly appeared in his refection on the water and then
quickly dissipated. He bent over the edge for a better look. Another
ripple appeared, dead-center, but whatever had caused it never came to
the surface. He watched in horror as he saw his compass slip, in slow
motion, from his pocket into the water. John desperately stared beyond
the surface of the lake, and leaned forward.

He hit the water with a muted splash. The shock of the cold lake
water engulfed him, flushing over his scalp and freezing every inch of
his skin. His strokes were long and slow – barely making a wave.

John circled, swimming with strong, freestyle strokes. His mind raced in all directions. He recalled teaching his little brother how to swim in the pond when they were boys back in Chicago. John could still feel his grip as he pried William's frightened little fingers away from his arm. He listened as his voice played his words back. "Will, let yourself float like a starfish."

Then he heard the laughter in Will's voice, later, as they played in the water. He smiled.

John surfaced for a moment, and then suddenly dived down as deep as he could. The water was cloudy, making it hard to see more than eerie outlines of what lay below.

He relived the morning he met Katie at the river, and how she had been his everything; she was the love of his life. If only he could stare into her beautiful eyes again and forget the battles that surrounded him.

And the *Compass Rose*; his pride and joy. He loved that vessel and its crew as if they were part of his family. Was there something he should have done differently? Something that might have changed its path? Was it his fault?

They were all gone. He felt a twist in his gut. The memories transformed into tiny knives stabbing at his heart.

Renewed misery hit him, and he thought again about finishing himself off in the lake, regardless of where that would have sent him; Heaven, Hell, Purgatory. Because, really, what was there if he didn't get Katie back?

The water was even colder the farther down he went, sapping his strength. His mind grew foggy and his thoughts became disjointed.

Images of his life, of Katie – and of Will's life … all of those men who would never return home to their own families, surrounded him. He suddenly jackknifed into the water.

Another bite of cold took his breath away. Captain Stockton began exhaling all of his air. His mouth opened on a gush of water. His lungs burned. The instinct rose to fight, but he clamped it down and let his body sink.

He mourned Katie's death again; she had so much she wanted to do; so much she never had the chance to finish. He felt his muscles relax; he became oddly calm as his imagination conjured up new tricks to play on him.

A flash of light momentarily illuminated his murky surroundings, cruelly teasing John with ghostly images of the men onboard the

*Compass Rose*; their frantic faces as they fought the inevitable. He saw Will's eyes, silently pleading with him, the sensation of Mr. Hale's grip on his arm, dragging him.

Too weak to fight, he couldn't help being haunted by voices all around him like black gulls calling him, repeating his name over and over again. The cold, dark wings of loss wrapped around John, freezing him all the way to his soul. The last conscious thought before the lake swallowed him, was of Katie.

And then it all went black.

## ~ Sixty-Eight ~

ZACHARY WATSON REACHED the edge of the dock, then threw his line out into the cool Erie water so that it cast the tiniest sliver of a spider web across the air. Within a minute, he had a nibble. He smiled. It had been a good day.

He inspected his hook and cast one more time.

Beyond the rocks, a large wave was building and finally broke as another approached from behind. The old fisherman stood and climbed the ridge, facing the clapboard house across the field and prepared to return home for supper, when he realized he'd left his hat on the beach.

He paused, bucket swinging from his hand. Peering over the embankment, he spotted the hat. Luckily, the wind hadn't taken it too far and it hadn't blown into the surf. But when he climbed back down the ridge to retrieve it, his eyes were drawn to a heap at the bottom of the wall.

There was something laying in the sand - something that hadn't been there yesterday. Slowly shaking his head, he took a slight detour to investigate what they had done this time.

It wouldn't be the first time that those hooligans covered large chunks of driftwood with old clothing, leaving them there to scare the young women who walked along the shore in the mornings as they gathered rocks and shells.

It was a cloudless afternoon. He secured the hat on his head and he snagged the first long twig he could find and approached the pile of clothing. But before he had the chance to poke the mound, he jumped backward.

It moved. The stick fell from his hand. He inched closer and picked up a thin branch, still sporting a few dead leaves. His scalp prickled. A shiver ran down his spine, his heart pumping like a steam engine.

He leaned over, his hat brimming with fishing hooks still on his head, and he cautiously nudged the heap.

* * *

He dropped the wood in a pile beside the fireplace, pulled out a box of matchsticks, and lit a fire.

Zachary returned thirty minutes later with a bowl of soup. Fire crackled. A branch of kindling tumbled onto the hearth, its tip ablaze. He tossed it back into the flames and turned his attention to the man he'd just dragged in from the beach.

The man stretched his feet out, under the blanket and wiggled his toes in front of the glow. His nose prickled. He scratched it and rolled onto his side.

"I'm Zachary. But you can call me Zach."

There was no reply.

He smiled, reaching for a twig at the top of the pile and cracking it, tossing the pieces into the fire. He leaned over the man, the corners of his mouth turned up. "This is the part where you tell me your name."

Still no reply.

Zach stood. "I suppose it's too soon for you." He brushed the knees of his trousers. "I am turning in for the night – I must be up by 4 am – before the fish." Just before he reached the doorway, he turned around and smiled. "Your supper is on the table. I'll see you in the morning."

* * *

When he peeked around the doorway in the morning, he saw the man was gone. Zachary sighed with disappointment and walked into the kitchen.

There he found his houseguest, tidying up the kitchen. The dishes had been washed and dried, and he had already begun the task of cleaning the fish from the previous days' catch.

"I cannot stay unless I find a way to pay you for your generosity and kindness toward me. Tell me, is there a way I can earn my keep?"

"That depends. How good are you at fishing?"

## ~ Sixty-Nine ~

THE LATE AFTERNOON SUN broke through the tunnel of trees, warming his back, as he made his way past the neat, tidy cottages that lined the little fishing village burrowed at the base of the cliffs.

Zachary looked up as the screen door creaked open. He could see by the look in his eyes that he was ready to move on.

With mixed feelings, Zachary stood and waited for him to speak. It had been eighteen months since the stranger washed up on his shore. And although they didn't always see eye-to-eye in the beginning, Zachary had come to enjoy the company of the man who called himself Elliott.

Suffering from amnesia, the man spent most of the first two months close to Watson's cottage, doing chores around the house. The turning point came when Zach asked him if he wanted to go out on his boat with him. The light in his eyes changed and Zach knew he was remembering.

Although Elliott and his previous life remained largely a mystery, Zach had been able to pull a few stories out of him – enough information to surmise that he had spent a good portion of his life on the water. And that he'd been tormented by something that had happened in his life.

Lucky for him, Elliott had been outstanding at fishing, helping Zach net more marketable fish during the last year or so, than he'd ever thought possible. But more than that, he'd been a good friend; somebody to talk to."

"I cannot thank you enough for your kindness and generosity toward me. You gave me a job." He stuffed the last shirt into the duffle bag and buckled the straps. "You shared your home with me Zachary, when you knew absolutely nothing about me or my past life."

"I knew that somewhere under all that ice a fire still burned. You were going through a very painful time. And I knew you would talk about it when you were ready."

Elliott met his eyes. "My family needed me ... But somehow, I never managed to be there for anybody. I was too busy with my own life."

Zach inhaled and breathed out. "I suspect that you are exaggerating, Elliott. It's only human nature to look through a magnifying glass when it comes to our own faults. But you will find a way to get past it." Then he patted him on the back and they walked out to the front porch together.

Elliott held his hand out in an invitation to a handshake. When he pulled back his hand afterward, there were three folded Canadian ten-dollar bills in his palm.

The older man laughed. "Don't you even think about returning that. Go on now – I want to watch you put it in your pocket." He grinned as the money found its way into the pocket of Elliott's trousers.

Elliott felt a grateful smile fighting its way to his lips. "Thank you Zachary."

"We are all sinners to one degree or another, aren't we?" A ghost of a smile flitted across Zach's face, tightening his wrinkles with its expression. "Life goes on whether you choose to move forward and take a chance in the unknown or stay behind, locked in the past, thinking of what could have been."

Elliott took three steps, and then pivoted quickly with a wave.

Zachary returned the gesture and watched him disappear in the first dip of the road back into town.

# ~ Seventy ~

*October, 1928*

THE CAR WAS DARK, but his face was illuminated in a sliver of early morning sunlight from the crack in the door.

He stood, slid the door open all the way and leaped from the moving train about a half mile from the outskirts of Cleveland, just as it began its approach from the west to the trestle bridge extending over the flats. He slammed hard to the ground, and then tucked in his head as he rolled down the embankment, his duffle close behind.

Over the course of two weeks, he had become proficient at bouncing from boxcar to boxcar. Although there was a constant threat and he was always in the face of danger, once he had set his sights on Cleveland, there was no turning back.

Exiting the train before it entered Cleveland-proper was a calculated move on his part. Although it was highly improbable, he couldn't run the risk of anyone recognizing him. His shaking hands, tanned, scarred and weathered from the sun, reached up and ran through his disorderly salt-and-pepper hair as he stood.

He leaned forward and tried in vain to stretch the kinks out of his aching back. Breathing into his hands, he tucked them inside his sleeves and looked around.

He was hit with a sudden wave of dizziness. This was a Cleveland that didn't feel at all familiar to him. Two years quickly morphed into more like ten; he felt like an immigrant arriving into the city for the first time.

Barges floated down the Cuyahoga River, stopping to load and unload crates of freight, some fresh from the assembly lines.

The heat of summer and the rainbow of fall had passed, leaving a day of bright blue skies and a breeze that carried the lingering scent of burning leaves and the promise of a Cleveland winter.

He walked. And he walked.

When he reached about halfway down the street, the light in his eyes changed. He stared at the house. Memories began flowing back to him.

Well-tended rose gardens framed either side of the floor-to-ceiling windows. He paused and stared at the front door as if he might catch a glimpse of his former self, arriving home. He turned to face the lake, dotted with steam freighters and ferryboats, beyond the beach.

Trying his best to distract himself, he passed the circular drive and kept walking.

✦✦✦✦✦✦✦✦✦✦✦

Jacques Laurent was weeding in the garden, swearing in French at the withered little weeds as he plucked them out, one-by-one. He grabbed a fistful of grass and yanked it from the earth, scattering the dirt like confetti.

As he leaned down to uproot another weed, he noticed a dark shape on the grass beside him in the late October afternoon sunlight. As the shadow increased in size, goosebumps invaded his skin.

No words were said, but Jacques turned around and was met by a man with a bag. Overgrown beard, disheveled coat and pants, the weathered fellow wobbled closer. Jacques couldn't speak. So the man spoke for him.

"Jacques." His throat was dry. He needed a drink.

Jacques knew in an instant who he was by his eyes. It was John. Captain John Stockton.

"Captain?" Jacques breathed.

He reached out and caught the captain as he nearly collapsed. John smiled weakly and nodded, with relief that he had been recognized. His eyes bored into Jacques' eyes. He inhaled deeply, and then exhaled.

"Jacques, I need your help." He staggered back a few steps as if he had been dealt a blow to the head. Then he rolled his eyes heavenward and wavered again.

Jacques wrapped his arms around John and guided him toward the house.

"Everyone believes you are dead, captain." Jacques said as he assisted John up the steps and into the cottage, then to the sofa in the parlor, where he collapsed again. Jacques quickly poured a glass of water and helped the captain hold it to his lips as he guzzled it.

John laid there a little while longer, then he probed. "Adele?"

Jacques slowly shook his head. "She was horrified and sickened at the news of your death." He looked out the window. "Our arguments became more and more frequent." His head tilted downward. "She went back to Paris."

"But what about your child?"

"Franklin lives with Adele, most of the time."

He smiled. "You and Adele will find each other again, Jacques – I am confidant of that."

"Would you like to go to your home, captain? It is just as you left it." Jacques asked him after a few minutes, but he had already fallen asleep.

John slept for hours, Jacques checking on him every now and again, to be sure he was breathing.

## ~ *Seventy-One* ~

"NO! *ABSOLUTELY NO DOCTORS!* I will remain ... dead." He turned away. The sound reverberating in the small confines of the little bedroom made John's voice seem almost venomous. Jacques wasn't sure how to react.

After a few deep breaths, John winced and faced Jacques again. He tried to smile apologetically, but it came across as more of a grimace.

"Anonymous."

Jacques saw the pain and uncertainty in the captain's eyes.

Captain Stockton's ear had become so infected that he was burning up with fever and drifting in and out of consciousness.

Jacques' backside was numb from sitting too long, sick himself, with worry. He leaned over and replaced the cold compress across John's forehead with a fresh one.

"Captain?" No response.

"John? Can you hear me?" Nothing.

Wringing his hands, Jacques made a decision – a decision that would undoubtedly send the captain into a rage once he found out, but he had no choice. An angry friend was better than a dead one. He quietly picked up the telephone receiver and waited for the operator's voice to come on the line.

"Please connect me with Doctor Tripp; Doctor Allen Tripp. Thank you."

✦✦✦✦ ✦✦✦✦✦✦ ✦✦✦

"You are quite the artist with the brush, Mr. Laurent," the doctor said as he studied the paintings that adorned the walls of Jacques Laurent's cottage. He moved from painting to painting, in awe. He walked past the open doorway to the tiny bedroom, finding himself drawn to a painting of a street in Paris on the opposite wall. But the moment he passed the doorway, he dropped his medical bag and darted into the room. Completely astonished, he froze.

Jacques headed him off before he could get too close. He shushed him. "He's sleeping."

"*Good* --" he lowered his voice to what amounted to a screaming whisper as he neared the captain's bedside. "*Good God* man – I thought John Stockton was long dead." He raked his hands through his wiry, white hair. "This changes everything - *Everything!*"

With wobbly legs, he dropped to a chair, then quickly sprang back up, as if he had just sat on red-hot coals. "Of course I will treat him. But we must notify the proper authorities!" He ran for the door into the hallway.

Jacques jumped into the doctor's path. They were nose-to-nose. "I told the captain that no one would find out he is alive."

"That's plain crazy! Now, if you will just step aside ..."

Sweat was pouring down Jacques Laurent's face. His fingers dug into Allen's arm, cutting off the circulation. His eyes darkened. After several seconds, he pinched the bridge of his nose.

He shot the doctor a warning look. "He wishes to remain anonymous." Drawing back his fist, Jacques prepared to let the punch fly. "I gave my word."

"Bah! Your word means *nothing* in this case!"

Tripp flew backward and hit the floor. He shook his head and then he grinned up at Jacques. "I deserved that."

A rainbow of emotions crossed both of their faces; neither knew if the other was about to laugh or cry. Jacques helped the doctor up and into a chair. He leaned back in the seat with a heavy sigh. Then he barked out a laugh but quickly stifled it.

Air ballooned in Jacques' cheeks. That hadn't gone well.

Dr. Tripp glanced back at Captain Stockton and his face softened. "Perhaps we can do something." He stood and walked to the window, staring silently out at the lake for a few minutes. He turned to Jacques and, in a voice just over a whisper, said, "It wouldn't be as if we were breaking the law …"

Jacques slowly stood and joined the doctor. They both turned back, facing the sleeping man on the other side of the room.

"No sir – I do not believe so."

"His infection has overtaken portions of his body other than his ear. It will take some time, but I think we can bring him back to reasonable health." He snapped his bag shut. "I am giving him something to fight the infection, and also something for the pain. I will return in the morning."

Jacques sat in the chair beside the bed.

"Mr. Laurent, you need to get some rest, physically and mentally, or you will not be able to care for John." He saw the look of determination on Jacques' face, nodding off, at John's side.

He put his bag back down on the table. "It's a lucky thing that I am an old man, with no family." He smiled. "I will remain here, until you have gotten a decent sleep."

Jacques awoke to the sound of a graphite pencil scratching across paper. Dr. Tripp was making notes – notes about the possible ways they could keep Captain Stockton "buried."

A blaze of challenge shot through Allen Tripp's eyes as he studied the captain through the mirror.

First, they must find an attorney. Not just any attorney – someone with an open mind; someone who could be trusted.

They needed a plan.

The silence in the room was filled with the sound of a ticking clock. Jacques could hear it from the hallway.

Slipping over to the door, Jacques opened it just a slight crack to hear better. He let go of the doorknob, but the slope of the room caused the door to open all the way, resting against the mirror.

Jacques Laurent knocked on the frame of the open door. "I do not wish to disturb you, but I was wondering if you have come up with a plan yet? We don't have much time." He observed the still reflection of Captain Stockton, in the bed across the room. He had yet to demonstrate any signs of improvement, except for the absence of the fever.

Allen Tripp and the attorney, Noah Trapp, contemplated among themselves, heads together, oblivious to the question."

Jacques entered the room. The smell of the surviving roses, two doors away, drifted in through the slightly open window by John's bedside.

"Doctor Tripp?"

Neither looked up. They continued debating among themselves.

Jacques tried again. "Mr. Trapp?"

They ignored him. He approached them. Jacques raised his voice in a desperate effort to get their attention.

***"Tripp! ... Trapp!"***

Dr. Tripp and Mr. Trapp, both startled, stared up at him.

Jacques cleared his throat and raised his index finger. "May I say something?"

Noah Trapp heaved a sigh and hesitated. But before Jacques could say anything, a weak voice from across the room broke the silence.

"Who the hell are *Tripp and Trapp?*"

Noah Trapp dropped his pencil. In unison, the trio of heads turned in the direction of the bed by the window.

The man in the bed stirred a little, and then he grumbled. "Sounds like a bad vaudeville act to me." He cracked an eyelid.

Then he opened his eyes.

266

## ~ Seventy-Two ~

THE AFTERNOON FADED into evening. The seventh draft of the plan was ready for John's approval. Mr. Trapp pushed the document across the bedside table in his direction.

The captain's eyes darted over the paper with the speed of a runaway car. He tapped his finger on the line spelling out the protection of his anonymity and pressed his lips together in a grim frown. "No good."

With great exaggeration, Noah slapped the remaining papers down onto the table next to him and stood.

The jangle of the telephone interrupted them, sending the attorney out into the hallway. Dr. Tripp sat next to John. He measured his words.

"You can't reject all of them. John, we are doing our best to give you everything you are asking for, but you've got to work with us a little."

John shot him a questioning frown.

In the end, John's argument won out. It was a difficult task, given the strict requirements each participant had insisted upon, but by midweek they had finally devised a plan that everyone was relatively happy with, including a mysterious, sizeable and untraceable Canadian bank account, opened for a Mr. Zachary Watson.

He rested his weathered hands on the arms of the chair. A comfortable house, a quiet room, magnificent streaks of orange and rose littering the sky; it just was not enough.

The captain stood and met his own reflection in the warped full-length mirror. The scars on his face had begun to fade, and were almost unnoticeable under his impeccably maintained beard.

His tears fell as his voice cracked. "I just couldn't come home to John Stockton's empty life." He turned away and back toward the window. "And I fear I still cannot."

The doctor gripped his shoulder, holding him in an embrace for just a moment. "John, you will find a way to make this work. Have faith."

Just before he went through the door, Noah Trapp shook his hand, a little less emotional but with just as much sincerity. "Find yourself something new to think about; something to help you remember all the good things in your life."

After Dr. Tripp and Mr. Trapp had gone, John sat, alone on the damp top step leading to Edgewater Beach. The sun had long dropped behind the horizon, but it didn't matter. He felt close to Katie, remembering being there with her, no matter what time of day or night it was.

John was staring up at the half-moon beneath the speckles of stars in the clear sky when he felt Jacques' hand on his shoulder.

"Captain, I think you should come back now. You are still weak and you must be careful."

He swallowed hard and nodded. He wasn't sure how long he had been there, but Jacques was right – he needed to take better care of himself – especially if he was going to successfully carry out Katie's wishes and dreams.

There were only three days left before Cleveland would be introduced to the caretaker who would be in charge of the Stockton estate. John was nervous. He hadn't even been in the house since he had left, more than two years ago.

Was it going to work? Would everyone buy the story?

Jacques sat beside the captain and unfolded a paper he had tucked in his pocket. He smoothed out the wrinkles, and held it against his chest.

"This was given to me a few years ago by someone very dear; very wise." He inhaled and blew out a soft breath. "I, too, had been going through a difficult time in my own life." Jacques stood and stepped down four stone slabs. He turned back to face Stockton. "These words have helped me, on many occasions, to continue; to keep things in perspective. I want you to have it."

He stepped back up to where John was sitting and he held out the paper. John stood and took it from Jacques with trembling fingers.

The captain quickly fell back onto the step; he recognized the handwriting immediately. That handwriting brought with it the kind of deep-seated peace he hadn't felt in years.

The words on the paper read:

*"Purpose is the reason you journey - Passion is the fire that lights your way."*

Another line had been added, beneath it, in Jacques handwriting:

*"It doesn't have to die."*

## ~ Seventy-Three ~

JOHN STOCKTON FIDDLED with the object in the pocket of his cardigan sweater before removing it. The face of his new watch reflected in the sunlight as he studied it. He snapped it shut.

The captain faced the warmth of the sun as he stood on the rocky cliffs along Edgewater.

A refreshing breeze greeted him as he faced the lake. He laughed, the sound rippling through his childhood memories with Will. It was a good laugh. For a moment, John felt the affection of Katie's hand there, on his.

A newfound feeling of peace washed over him. This journey of his wasn't finished yet. He had much to accomplish. There was work to be done.

He took in a deep breath, opened the watch again and caught a glimpse of himself reflecting off the glass.

Elliott Hutchinson smiled back at him.

It was time.

www.ingramcontent.com/pod-product-compliance
Lightning Source LLC
Chambersburg PA
CBHW020820260626
47169CB00003B/757